Margery Hollis

Through Thick and Thin

Vol. 2

Margery Hollis

Through Thick and Thin
Vol. 2

ISBN/EAN: 9783337213206

Printed in Europe, USA, Canada, Australia, Japan

Cover: Foto ©Andreas Hilbeck / pixelio.de

More available books at **www.hansebooks.com**

Through Thick and Thin.

By
Margery Hollis,
Author of
"Anthony Fairfax,"
"Audrey."

In Three Volumes.

Vol. II.

London:
Richard Bentley & Son,
Publishers in Ordinary to Her Majesty the Queen.
1893.

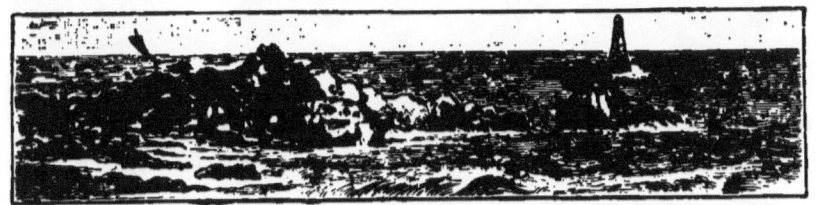

CONTENTS OF VOL. II.

THROUGH THICK AND THIN.

CHAPTER I.

A PEACEFUL HOME.

"A world of happy wonders in one smile."
A. LANG.

IT was an afternoon in December. The sun had set and the dusk was gathering. It was too dark to see comfortably, and Mrs. Mildmay put down the novel she was reading. She did not ring for lamps at once. She was in no great hurry to know how the story ended, for her mind was pleasantly engaged at that moment with real life, and she was in the state of lazy well-being when one grudges even the exertion of changing one's position. It was too much trouble to rise to ring the bell. So she lay back in her low chair and watched the glowing fire with a smile of placid content. Life had run very smoothly with her since she had taken possession of her new home, and nothing had so far taken the edge off the keenness of her enjoyment. She gratefully acknowledged herself to be one of the most fortunate of women.

The door opened, and Sophy turned her head towards it.   .

" Is that you, Gay ? "

"Yes; here are Jim and I," replied Gay. "We have had a long walk. This frost is delightful."

" It's going to last, too," said Jim, with
an important air. " William says so ; and
he always knows. The tarn at Tarn Hall
is bearing, and I want to go and skate on
it to-morrow. William says he will teach
me. May I go, mother ? "

" Yes, certainly, darling."

" I must have a pair of skates. Can't
William fetch me a pair from the village
to-night ? "

" Oh yes, dear," said Sophy, quickly.

Jim was quite satisfied with her absent
granting of his requests. He liked his
stepmother, for when he carried a petition
to her it was never denied ; and for
sympathy and interest in his small affairs
he looked to Gay, who gave them liberally.

" Oh, Gay," went on Sophy, in a more
animated manner, "what *do* you think ?
Miles is coming this afternoon, and his

housekeeper was in quite a state about it, for she has rheumatism badly, and she can hardly get about. She has only a young girl to help her just now—one of the Lawsons. She sent over to ask Porter if she could let her have something to make out a dinner for Miles to-night, and Porter, of course, came to me about it. I thought poor Miles would be too uncomfortable, with Mrs. Mason crippled and Nelly Lawson waiting on him, so I sent him a note, begging him to stay with us. It will be nicer for him, and I know James will like to have him. He will be here in half an hour now. Would you mind looking at his room—he is to be in the blue-room —to see if it is all right? Sarah is very good and careful, but servants forget things sometimes."

"Yes, dear; I'll see to it," replied Gay.

She ran lightly upstairs to the blue-room, where close inspection revealed that nothing that could make a guest comfortable was lacking, and then she went to her own room to lay aside hat and jacket. She lingered over that business, trying to subdue the fluttering of her pulses which Sophy's intelligence had caused.

To know that she would so soon meet Miles Thornburgh, sent her mind back to the last times she had seen him, especially to that evening at the Kemble, of which her memory retained a very sharp impression. It was a recollection that was not agreeable to her, quite apart from the peculiarly painful circumstances with which it was associated. She did not like to remember how she had felt about him then; she was ashamed of her pleasure in his presence and of her belief in his admiration and liking.

When the glow of that evening's *exalté* mood had faded, she blamed herself severely for such a flight of fancy, and determinedly set forth the reasons against indulging in such folly. She was resolved not to expect much from life in any way. Her shrewdness and knowledge of the world made her rate her claims very low, and pride showed her that to cherish sanguine hopes of the future was to court mortification.

She did not believe in romance—at least, not where she was concerned. Experience had made her cynical, and broken the spring of youthful confidence in her. It was only silly to dream of a lover's devotion. "I have not had a proper upbringing," she reflected dis-

passionately. "Why, when I was fifteen
I knew more of debt and mean shifts than
he will know if he lives to be ninety. I
have rubbed against all sorts of people
while I tried to keep body and soul
together. I have been hungry because
I couldn't buy food; I have had to take
charity. And it isn't as if I had great
beauty to make a man overlook my draw-
backs. I am not even particularly
good-looking. A pretty match I should
be!"

Besides, there was another reason for
banishing all fond fancies—a reason that
was known only to Gay. The cloud
which had threatened to darken all her
sky had disappeared for the time, but it
was always possible that it might return.
She did not now go in fear of that. Two
months had passed quietly and she felt

secure from discovery. But, so long as she knew that discovery was not altogether impossible, so long it would not be right to let any man unite his fortunes to hers. She had not said so much definitely to herself. In the reaction after that episode in London, it had seemed to her too improbable that Thornburgh's liking had been more than was enough to make him disposed to flirt a little, for her to consider the possibility of anything really serious.

She had not been by any means unhappy on his account, and none of her time had been wasted in dreams and longings. Such conduct would have been in her opinion ridiculous. As she expected little from life she was the more easily contented, and she had found life very good that autumn. So long as she could dwell in

Sophy's home and see Sophy happy and prosperous, it would be wicked to repine.

She had been so serenely cheerful that it provoked her a little to find that the prospect of Thornburgh's reappearance disturbed her calm. She was sorry that Sophy was hospitable to her cousin ; she would have preferred not to be thrown so much into his way. She took herself to task for these sentiments as she laid aside her walking gear. She had no romance about him—none. She was not going to fall in love with him. And there was little danger that she would see much of him. Sophy and Mr. Mildmay would claim his society, and she could easily keep herself in the background.

The lamps were lighted in the drawing-room when she went downstairs, and Mr. Mildmay was standing with his back to the fire, listening to his wife, who was discoursing in plaintive accents.

" I hope I have done right," she was saying when Gay entered, " but I feel quite uncomfortable about it now. It is about Miles, Gay. I wonder whether Adelaide will be offended because I asked him here. She always seems to lay claim to him, and she will probably think he ought to have gone there. I feel almost sure she won't be pleased. Adelaide doesn't like other people to do things— she wants to be first."

One of the luxuries of Sophy's prosperity was to indulge occasionally in disparaging criticisms of her sister-in-law. It was some indemnification for the unwelcome discipline which she had undergone at Mrs. Fletcher's hands.

" Never mind if she doesn't like it,"

said Mr. Mildmay, placidly. "What does it matter? But surely she can't be unreasonable enough to object to your inviting your cousin? He is as much your relation as hers."

"More," observed Sophy. "He is only related by marriage to Adelaide, you know. But she seems to think he is quite the property of Tarn Hall. You'll see she will get him away; he will soon go to stay there."

Mr. Mildmay appeared to be unmoved by this forecast. Sophy looked unhappy, and settled her bracelets with puckered brows.

"I do wish I hadn't sent that note to him," her plaint went on. "Adelaide will think me interfering. I believe she has a notion that Miles would do very well for Mabel."

"So he would," said Mr. Mildmay; "and she would do very well for him. She's a pretty girl, is Mabel, and a nice one too."

"Very likely he would rather have gone to Tarn Hall, if I had left him alone. I wish I had stopped to think——"

These heart-searchings were cut short by sounds of an arrival. Mr. Mildmay went out to receive his guest, and Sophy followed. There was a confusion of friendly greetings accompanied by wild barks from Fido, Jim's dog, a muddle-headed beast, who forgot old acquaintance, and barked as readily at accustomed visitors as at tramps.

As Sophy led her guest into the drawing-room, she reverted to her doubts, and plunged into an apology for inviting him.

"I thought you would be more com-

fortable here than at your house, Miles,"
she explained.

" That is quite certain, and I am deeply
grateful to you for taking me in, Sophy,"
returned her cousin, cordially. " How do
you do, Miss Rushton ? "

It was a brief, almost aside, greeting,
for Sophy demanded his attention ; but
the lowered tone said, " How glad I am
to see you ! " as plainly as explicit words.

" If Adelaide wants you," pursued Sophy,
" you must go to her—you must not think
of us ; we shall not be at all offended.
She will like to have you part of the time
you are in the north this Christmas."

" That sounds as if you repented already
of your invitation to Miles, and wanted to
cut his stay short, do you know, Sophy ? "
said her husband, laughing.

" Oh no, no, indeed ; I should like him

to stay as long as possible," protested Sophy; "and I hope you will, Miles. But, of course, you might like to give some time to Tarn Hall."

"Thank you; I shall be delighted to stay with you as long as Mrs. Mason is disabled," returned Thornburgh. "If you knew how rejoiced I was to get your note this afternoon, you would be afraid that I shall inflict myself unmercifully upon you."

Sophy beamed at this compliment, and gave no more consideration to Adelaide's possible sentiments about her daring attention to her cousin.

After tea, Jim, beautifully arrayed in violet velvet and a lace collar, came down for an hour in the bosom of the family. His attire had become much more picturesque and studied since his step-

mother had bought it. He attached himself to Gay, who was sitting a little apart,
and she began a game of cards with him.

Presently Thornburgh, who had been
held in talk by his host and hostess
since his arrival, went over to the pair
at the card-table, and asked what they
were playing at.

"Vingt-et-un," replied Jim.

"You seem to enjoy it very much,"
said Thornburgh. "Is it so engrossing,
Miss Rushton?"

"It is a delightful game," she returned.

"You can play, if you like, Cousin
Miles," said Jim, kindly, pausing in his
laborious and painstaking dealing.

"Thank you, Jim; I think I should
like to take a hand."

Jim was charmed with his cousin that
evening; he had never before found him

such a congenial companion. Game after game did he join in, showing unwearied sympathy for Jim's very bad luck.

Once Sophy interposed.

" Miles, don't let Jim trouble you. You must not put yourself out of your way for his amusement."

" Oh, I am playing for my own amuse- ment—I am enjoying myself," returned Thornburgh.

Jim was highly pleased with that speech, for the idea that people should play for his amusement galled his proud spirit.

" It is a jolly game," he said, smiling over the cards he was clutching in his dimpled hand.

His two playfellows looked at him with responsive smiles, and then their eyes met, and Gay looked down and studied her cards closely.

"Very jolly," said Thornburgh, in a heartfelt tone.

Next day was bright and clear; the frost was hard; and the chief topic discussed at breakfast was skating. Mr. Mildmay lamented that he must go to the nearest town on business, and envied Thornburgh.

"I'll drive you to Tarn Hall," he said; "of course you will want to begin as soon as you can."

"Thanks, yes; I should like to get there early. When shall you go, Sophy?"

Mrs. Mildmay was not going at all; she did not skate.

"Don't you skate, Miss Rushton?" asked Thornburgh.

"Very little."

"But surely you are not going to lose this splendid chance of learning more?"

" I think I shall go after lunch; I haven't time this morning," said Gay.

Owing to its high exposed situation the tarn in the grounds of Tarn Hall froze early, and it was therefore a favourite resort of the skaters of the neighbourhood. There were a good many people on the ice when Gay made her tardy appearance. She had driven over alone in a little pony-cart which had been used by Miss Mildmay, and was now made over to her service.

She stood for a moment on the bank of the lake, looking at the pretty scene, the glowing faces and swiftly moving figures against a background of firs. Thornburgh was skating with Mabel— just what she had expected to see. " They look very nice together; she is the right height to pair well with him, and how pretty she is with that bright colour and the sun on her hair!" said Gay to herself. Of course that was the right thing. She had seen from her first coming to the place how suitable it would be; and she impressed the eminent fitness of the arrangement afresh on her mind by way of wholesome self-discipline.

All the skaters were engaged with their pastime and their companions, and nobody noticed Gay's approach at first. She beckoned to William, the groom, who was looking after Jim, and asked him to put her skates on. William fetched a chair for her, and while he buckled the straps Jim stood by, and delivered a prolix account of his experiences on the ice.

"I do it very well," he remarked, with satisfaction. "William says I am learning fast, and he's going to teach me to do figures soon.   *You* can't do them, Gay."

" I certainly cannot—to keep on my feet used to be about all I could do," returned Gay, smiling.

"William can teach you," suggested Jim.   "You will, won't you, William ? "

" I'd be proud to do anything for Miss Rushton, Master Jim," replied William ; '' but she will have better teachers than me."

"Oh, you do them quite beautifully," declared Jim, eager to defend William, who was his great friend and ally, from any misjudgment caused by his too modest estimate of his own powers.

As William finished, Thornburgh came up, and, much to Jim's indignation, insisted on examining Gay's skates for himself.

"William fastened them—they're all right," protested Jim, warmly.

"My dear Jim," said his cousin, "suppose you go and skate." And William drew his young champion away with gentle, resistless force.

"What are you smiling at?" asked Jim, when he drew breath after the long run.

"Little boys shouldn't ask questions," was the unsatisfactory reply.

"Is it because you think Cousin Miles foolish to make such a fuss about the fastenings?"

"No, Master Jim, I think Mr. Thornburgh is very sensible," rejoined the magnanimous William.

Sophy called at Tarn Hall that afternoon, and found her sister-in-law in the drawing-room with two or three matrons whose young people were on the ice. Mrs. Fletcher proposed that they should go to the lake to see the skaters and summon them to tea, and the ladies set forth, exchanging as they went the stock remarks about skating—it was so healthy, such good exercise, so graceful, "and," added one, "it brought young people together."

This remark was addressed to Sophy, and she acquiesced with a yawn behind her muff. That was a process in which she took no interest at that moment; she was longing for tea, and thinking it inconsiderate that Adelaide had delayed that important meal to walk a quarter of a mile in the keen air to see a handful of people skating. The most graceful movements on the ice would not give her so much pleasure as the sight of a plate of hot muffins borne towards her.

She looked on listlessly while her companions admired the scene on the tarn, only exerting herself so far as to say something civil about Mabel. Sophy girded in her own mind at Mrs. Fletcher's maternal pride; but she could not avoid flattering it at times—there was something in her sister-in-law's complacency which exacted acknowledgment that it was well founded.

"She skates very nicely," said Sophy; "and how well she looks! But where is Miles?"—in a tone of surprise, as she observed that Mabel's attendant was not that gentleman.

"It would hardly do for Miles to be always with Mabel," said Mrs. Fletcher, with a smile. "There he is, looking after

Gay. I am glad of that; there are a good many people here to-day that are almost strangers to her, and I should be sorry for her to feel neglected. Miles is always thoughtful."

Mrs. Fletcher spoke in perfect simplicity. She did not mean to patronize Gay, nor to insinuate that attention to her must be disinterested. The speech was certainly open to that construction; but the observer who noted in it feminine spite would have erred grossly. It was only dictated by stupidity, which perhaps is commoner than spite. Nothing is denser than a placid assurance of the superiority of one's self and one's belongings; in all good faith Mrs. Fletcher believed that Thornburgh was unselfishly thoughtful in taking notice of Gay, and was glad of his kindness to the poor guest.

Thornburgh's benevolence seemed to bring him a good deal of enjoyment; he was bending over his companion with an engrossed look and talking in an animated fashion. Something in the attitude of the two figures—in the turn of Gay's head as she glanced up and smiled, in the way Thornburgh was holding her hands— struck Sophy, and she looked hard at them. A new light suddenly fell on the remark that skating brought young people together. These young people seemed to be turning the occasion to account. How charming Gay looked with her shining eyes and that faint shy smile!

Sophy was in very high spirits for the rest of her visit, and chatted with unflagging vivacity to her fellow-guests during tea.

"She was quite the life of the party," said Mrs. Steele, afterwards.

Clara, with the crude frankness of a youthful relation, remarked that Aunt Sophy talked louder than anybody else in the room, and was as excited as if she had been skating herself.

When Sophy rose to go, she made her way to Thornburgh, who was talking to one of the older ladies, and offered him a seat in her carriage.

"Many thanks, but I have begged a seat from Miss Rushton," he said.

"Very well," said Sophy, smiling as sweetly as though she rejoiced to escape his company for the drive.

Mrs. Fletcher was near, and her instinct for management was roused.

"You would be much more comfortable with Sophy, Miles," she remarked. "Miss Rushton has the pony-cart, and there is not much room in it."

"Oh, there is room enough for me, surely," said Thornburgh, laughing. "I am not gigantic, and I don't like driving in a close carriage. Shall I be very much in your way, Miss Rushton?"

Gay had come up to take leave of her hostess.

"Not at all," she returned, in a manner which struck Mrs. Fletcher as slightly out of place. She spoke graciously and amiably, as if she was conferring a favour, and she was not important enough to take that tone with Miles Thornburgh. "We shall be honoured by your company, Jim and I," she added, smiling.

Mrs. Fletcher went to the hall door with Sophy, and her sense of fitness was further wounded. While Sophy found many last words to say on the steps, Thornburgh was showing a deep interest in Gay's comfort. He tucked the rug round her with superfluous care, and expressed dissatisfaction because she had not a foot-warmer.

"But I don't care for one on such a short drive," she protested.

"Good-bye, Adelaide dear," said Sophy, kissing her sister-in-law with effusive affection. "I'm *so* sorry to hear about poor old Mrs. Lawson, and I will send her some soup to-morrow, poor thing!"

Mrs. Fletcher gazed in some wonder at Sophy's expression of profound satisfaction; it seemed hardly the right look to wear after the melancholy account she had just been giving of Mrs. Lawson's sufferings. But Sophy was flighty.

That evening, after dinner, Mr. Mildmay, as usual, asked Gay to sing. Thornburgh placed himself near her, and there was a little low-toned talk between the songs. Presently Mr. Mildmay, also as usual, fell into a peaceful doze, overcome by the heat of the fire and the soothing influence of Gay's voice. Then the singing came to an end, and the talk was carried on steadily.

Sophy read a novel with languid attention, glancing every now and then over the volume at the two by the piano, with a smile at their absorbed air, and exercising a really heroic self-control in keeping silence. She infinitely preferred chat to reading ; but, though a score of things occurred to her that she would have liked to say, she kept them back. Not for worlds would she come in Gay's way.

CHAPTER II.

IN A HOLIDAY MOOD.

" Her eyes make bright the uneventful days."
The Earthly Paradise.

NEXT morning Sophy had a cold, and breakfasted in bed, a little indulgence which she was always glad to have an excuse for. She had not finished her leisurely meal when Gay appeared with inquiries after her health. Sophy made light of her indisposition. It was not much of a cold—just enough to cause her to feel lazy.

"The frost is as hard as ever, isn't it?" she said.

" Oh yes ; it is very cold."

" That's right. I am glad the frost is holding. You must go earlier to the ice than you did yesterday."

" I think I shall not go to-day. I will stay with you, Sophy. It will be dull for you to be alone."

Sophy exclaimed at this proposal, declared that solitude had charms for her, as for sages, and that she could not allow Gay to lose her pleasure.

"You did enjoy it yesterday, didn't you?"

" Yes," Gay acknowledged, in a subdued tone, " I enjoyed it very much."

" You will never skate well if you don't practise as much as possible," said Sophy ; " and I insist upon your going."

" But it isn't a positive necessity or a moral obligation that I *should* skate well," represented Gay.

" Whatever is worth doing is worth doing well," Sophy remarked gravely. " I don't need you at all. I have plenty of books—Mudie's box came yesterday— and I shall doze all the afternoon ; for I am always sleepy when I have a cold. Go and put on your things to be ready to start with James. He said he should order the dog-cart for half-past nine."

" I must order dinner—— "

" I will see to that. Just write down what you intended to have, and I will give the paper to Porter. There is some paper in the blotting-book there. Gay, I will have you go," said Sophy, with a fine air of authority.

Gay laughed—the energetic tone was comical in Sophy's voice—and obediently wrote out the bill of fare.

" I *think* Miles is better off for food

here than he would be at Tarn Hall," said Sophy, with an air of satisfaction, when she had read the *menu*. "Adelaide's dinners were very monotonous. She is very narrow. I got quite tired of seeing the same things so often, didn't you, Gay? I like variety myself. Yes, this is a very nice dinner, thank you, dear. But don't stay here any longer. Go and put on your things at once. James can't bear to be kept waiting."

Gay went to her room and made a rapid toilet. The night before, as she reviewed the events of the day, she had reproached herself for laxity in carrying out her intention of avoiding Thornburgh. She had begun well, and could contemplate the first half of the day with satisfaction; but the end had not been after that beginning. As soon as she got to the ice she had been obliged to do what she meant not to do—what she wished not to do—and the rest of the day had belonged to Thornburgh.

He had taken possession of her, and it had been so pleasant that she had for· gotten her sage resolutions; so pleasant that in her meditations she was startled by a sense of danger. It would never do to let herself care much for his society, she reflected, as she sat over her fire. It would never do to let her liking for him grow into her master. She shrank from love; she knew it would be cruel to her.

She would be more careful; and as skating did not offer favourable conditions for the caution and self-control which she must exercise, she would keep away from the ice. She had slept on this determination, had carried it down to breakfast with her, and hailing Sophy's cold with gladness, had declared her intention of bearing the sufferer company. She had not been shaken in her purpose by Mr. Mildmay's kindly persuasions, nor by the vexation which Thornburgh made no attempt to hide. "If I am so sorry to disappoint him a little, and so glad that he is disappointed, it is high time I pulled up," she thought. "I can stop now ; but if I go on seeing much of him, I shall lose my feet—I shall *want* to be with him. And I must not let it come to that—I must not! Life is quite hard enough, without increasing its unpleasantness by love troubles."

But Sophy had driven her from that position of defence, and Gay was not sorry for it. She liked skating, and the weather was so fine. It would be pleasanter to be on the ice than sitting in a hot room with Sophy.   And she stifled the muttered warnings of prudence by the reflection that she probably would not see much of Thornburgh that day.   He could not neglect his relations—particularly Mabel.

Thornburgh and Jim were in the hall when she went down.   Jim was making his dog beg for lumps of sugar, and appealing for his cousin's admiration of Fido's one accomplishment.   Thornburgh was leaning against the table with a bored expression, casting a listless glance occasionally at the performance.

Suddenly his face cleared, and he made a step or two to meet Gay.

"You *are* going ? "

"Sophy insists upon it.   She won't have my company this morning," said

Gay, looking down at the glove she was buttoning.

" Dear Sophy!" murmured Thornburgh, with deep feeling. "She is my favourite cousin."

" Gay, look at Fido," Jim put in. " He begs beautifully now."

"Never mind Fido just now, Jim; I want you to wear this."

She fastened a fur tippet round the child's shoulders, while he wriggled and loudly remonstrated against her care.

" You're an ungrateful young shaver," said Thornburgh.

" You wouldn't like it yourself, if she put horrid tippets on you," growled Jim. " You wouldn't wear them."

" Indeed I would," returned Thornburgh, gravely. "If Miss Rushton ordered me to do a thing, I should do it."

"I know you wouldn't," said Jim, sceptically. "Gay, just tell him to do something, and see if he does it."

Gay shook her head and laughingly declined to make the experiment— Mr. Thornburgh was old enough to look after himself.

They found the Fletchers already on the tarn. The girls surrounded Thornburgh at once, asking questions, laying claim to him in their usual way, and thereby rousing a very unusual impatience in him. He answered their queries as quickly as he could, hastily promised to look at Mabel's skates, which, she said, were uncomfortable, and turned to see that Mr. Mildmay was putting on Gay's skates.

"Here, Mabel, let me see what is wrong," he said with resignation.

Gay skated for a little while with Mr.

Mildmay; then she joined Clara and Bridget, who were very glad of her company, and kept close at either side. She talked a great deal, and seemed quite engrossed with them.

Presently she was accosted by Mr. Ashton, the new curate. He was a tall, thin young man, with rather too high an estimate of his own consequence, which was based partly on his respect for his orders, partly on the respect of others for his private fortune. He had a good income already, and had large expectations, and he was naturally very well received by the world. His self-complacency did not make him stiff and proud; on the contrary, it made his manners, like those of Mr. and Mrs. Suckling of Maple Grove, " highly conciliating." He was very kind to those with whom he came in

contact, who presumably were less fortunate than himself.

He addressed Gay now with special
amiability. He had learnt only the day
before that she was a poor dependant on
Mr. Mildmay, and he was nobly determined that he would be as civil to her as
if she were Mr. Mildmay's daughter. His
affability met with a reward. Miss Rushton appreciated it ; she replied with animation, and he was drawn into a long talk.
He was specially interested at that
moment in getting up a series of parish
entertainments for the winter evenings,
and when he found that Miss Rushton was
musical, he freely poured himself out to
such an intelligent listener, and told her
what songs and readings he thought most
suitable for the people.

Gay was making a desperate effort to

carry on a losing fight. Defeat was imminent. Her conviction of that was growing clearer as she agreed with Mr. Ashton; but she would hold out as long as she could.

"We must have some comic songs," Mr. Ashton observed. "They are always liked. The difficulty is that so many comic songs are vulgar, and of course we could not have any of that kind."

"Oh, of course not," echoed Gay, mechanically. Aside she was saying: "I can't keep this up all day—it is impossible to be so rude. I must talk to him part of the time."

"I don't know," pursued her interlocutor, "whether there is anybody here that is good at comic songs. Do you know?"

"You will sing yourself, won't you?" returned Gay, still absently.

"Yes, I will help, certainly. But I don't sing comic songs, Miss Rushton."

She earnestly assured him that such an irreverent idea was far from her, and begged to know what songs he would favour the audience with. She listened sadly to his rejoinder; she was getting very tired of the talk.

"Hi, Gay, stop and look at me!" cried Jim, exultantly. "I can go alone quite well now."

She stopped with a smile, and Jim slowly bore down upon her, followed by the devoted Bridget.

"Little Mildmay is your cousin, is he not?" said Mr. Ashton.

"No, he is not my cousin. Mrs. Mildmay was my father's second wife," said Gay; "it is a rather complicated relationship."

Jim had reached them in time to hear Gay's answer.

"Gay is my sister," he said with pride. "I don't like cousins—they're no good at all; sisters are far jollier. Didn't I do that nicely, Gay? Come and skate with me—*I* will help you"—holding out his hand.

Mr. Ashton laughed, whereat Jim glared at him defiantly.

"Yes, I will come with you, dear," said Gay, taking the small hand.

"Well done, Jim," said Thornburgh, joining the little group, and patting the child's shoulder approvingly. "You are a gallant squire of dames. But you ought not to forsake Bridget; look after her, and I will help Miss Rushton, if she will let me."

"Bridget can come too," said Jim.

" That would be too much for you,"
returned Thornburgh, gravely, " and it
would be selfish of you too, Master Jim,
to keep so many ladies to yourself."

"Oh, if you *want* to skate with Gay——"

" That is just what I want, and she
has kept me waiting a long time." (Mr.
Ashton was at some distance now.) " I
thought you were never going to get rid
of that fellow "—aside to Gay.

" He was very kind in helping me," she
replied with dignity.

" He seems to me an insufferable
coxcomb—can't imagine how you could
tolerate him so long."

Jim's sharp ears had caught this brief
colloquy, low-toned as it was, and he
asked now with an air of interest—

" What is a coxcomb ? "

" Don't ask questions about things that

are not said to you," said Thornburgh, hastily.

" And why are you scolding Gay ? " Jim went on. " She hasn't been naughty."

Thornburgh looked a little confused at this close inquiry, and peremptorily ordered Jim off.

" I beg your pardon," he said, in a slightly constrained tone, when Jim and Bridget had gone. " I was rude, I fear— I don't know Mr. Ashton."

He had been gravely disturbed by the sight of Mr. Ashton's attentions to her, and a fit of jealous fright had seized him, lest he had done a very foolish thing in leaving the field clear the last two months. He had carried out the intention of staying in town till Christmas which he had announced when he went up after Sophy's wedding. He did not care to advertise the state of his feelings by rushing after Gay; he was in the mood in which it contented him to think of her and look forward. But now he asked with alarm what advantage might not that prosing curate have gained while he was absent.

"I think you are a little unfair to him," said Gay, looking before her with a smile. "He isn't a coxcomb. But he is a bore —I am quite sure of that."

Thornburgh looked at her with an expression of satisfaction. There was nothing to dread from Mr. Ashton.

"Come," was all he said, as he held out his hand.

She put hers into it, and glided on, forgetting all the danger that she knew lurked this way, forgetting everything but that life was holding a draught of pleasure to her lips. She drank it with the eager thirst of one that has been denied for long ; she could not forego it.

That day was the very brightest she had known in her twenty-three years. She did not look before or after; she simply gave herself up to the present. The mere sense of existence was delicious as she felt the physical exhilaration of the clear frosty sunlit air and the swift skimming over the ice ; and she was thrilled with a more subtle and potent delight by the presence of the man beside her.

Thornburgh did not devote himself too openly to her ; but he saw more of her than of anybody else, and Gay was quite content when he was paying atten-tion to other people. She knew that he would come back to her as soon as he could. Bridget and Jim profited by his duty absences. Then Gay joined them, and made herself very charming to them. The two children agreed privately that she was the best playmate they had, and felt hostile when they had to give her up.

At sunset she was racing with them, laughing as merrily as Jim, when Thornburgh drew near.

"Will you go round once more?" he asked. "Are you tired?"

"I am not tired at all; I will go with pleasure."

She spoke with the graciousness which Mrs. Fletcher had noticed yesterday, and disapproved of. Gay's pride would never have let her play the undignified part of the fluttering maiden, embarrassed by the consciousness of admiration and plainly grateful for it. Thornburgh liked the air of composed graciousness ; it suited her, and he was of Thackeray's mind—if he served a woman it must be on his knees.

"I must be off after this," he said, as they started on the round of the lake. "I have an article to finish to-day, and I want to get it done before dinner, so that I may hear some songs later. You will sing, won't you ?"

"Oh yes, of course. I sing every night. Mr. Mildmay likes music, and I like singing."

"Your voice has improved wonderfully since the summer. It was very good then, but it is delicious now—the tone is so full and sweet."

She looked pleased for a moment, then a shadow crossed her face.

"It is much stronger now," she said briefly.

"You must have been working hard to sing as you do."

"Yes, I have practised regularly ;" and she changed the subject.

A compliment to her singing did not come so gratefully to her ear now as in former days. She had worked diligently to bring her voice into as perfect condition as might be, as one would polish and sharpen a weapon for readiness in case of need, and as she remembered that possible necessity a chill of fear seized her. Oh, if it came *now*, how could she bear it ? She half drew her hand away from Thornburgh's. If that day came, she would have to stand alone.

"You are tired," he said. "You must not go any further."

She laughed a little nervously.

"I am tired. I have just found it out," she acknowledged.

He took her skates off and accompanied her to the house. Mrs. Fletcher was sitting alone by the fire.

"I have brought Miss Rushton in to get some tea, Adelaide," said Thornburgh. "She has done too much, I fear."

Mrs. Fletcher regretted Gay's fatigue, and ordered tea at once. She was "civil, civil as an orange," but she was annoyed. It really was foolish of Miles to make such a fuss about this girl. She was only a poor dependant, whose position was not any better than that of a governess, and she should not be encouraged to forget her proper place. She was not important enough to have tea at Tarn Hall earlier than usual on her account. Mrs. Fletcher had felt much less well-disposed towards Gay since the girl had ceased to be the recipient of her kindness.

Mabel came in, followed by Bridget and Jim, bringing a request that the skaters might have tea on the ice, as they were unwilling to leave it.

" Mr. Ashton says the ice is perfect," said Mabel, "and after tea he will show us how to do a quadrille on it. Cousin Miles, you will be one, won't you ? "

" I cannot, Mabel. I have some work to do before dinner, and I must be off straightway."

"Oh, I am sorry you must go. The quadrille will be fun. Mr. Ashton skates so well, mother."

" Cousin Miles doesn't like him," observed Jim. " He called him a coxcomb —you did, Cousin Miles, and you scolded Gay for talking to him."

"Oh, isn't he nice ? " said Mabel.

"You might have told me that, Cousin Miles. I am sure I wouldn't have talked to him if I had known."

She looked reproachfully at her cousin, aggrieved that he had not given her, as well as Gay, the benefit of his direction. There was no independence of spirit in Mabel. She always wanted a guide and protector.

"He isn't so bad as that," said Thornburgh, lightly. "My dislike of him doesn't go so far that I wish to have him sent to Coventry."

"Then why did you tell Gay not to talk to him?" demanded Jim, firmly.

"I *must* be going," said Thornburgh, affecting not to hear this query. "Good-bye, Mabel."

"But, do you think he isn't nice?" persisted Mabel, who was anxious to have this point cleared up. "Are his people not gentlefolks ?"

"So far as I know he may be connected with half the county families in England," returned Thornburgh. "He is nice enough. I spoke hastily before. If I had known that I should be brought so sternly to book, I should have governed my tongue better. But you must not accept Jim's report. He has a lively fancy at times, which makes him twist words sadly."

"Yes, indeed," said Gay, with a stern glance at the erring child.

"Mabel," observed Mrs. Fletcher, when she and her daughter were alone after dinner, "you shouldn't have kept Miles this afternoon, when he was in a hurry to get away."

"Why, mother, I only asked him a

question or two. I wanted to understand about Mr. Ashton."

" Yes, dear, but he didn't like being questioned. You might have seen that."

Mabel looked surprised. When her eyes widened and her lips parted in that way, her face had a somewhat blank expression. Her mother regarded her with less complacency than usual.

" I didn't notice," said Mabel.

" You must learn more tact, dear. It is very necessary for a woman. If she hasn't it, she may appear—stupid."

Mrs. Fletcher must have been much irritated before she could apply such an adjective to her daughter, and, indeed, her usual placid equanimity had been sadly shaken that afternoon. She had been displeased by Thornburgh's early departure, which his alleged reason did not at all excuse. He could very well make time later for his work.

Mrs. Fletcher, of course, held the popular theory that such an easy exercise as composition may be performed at any hour that suits the convenience of the writer's friends—Miles was sufficiently at home with the Mildmays to leave them in the evening if he liked, and the arrangement he had chosen signified that he preferred the society at Westby Lodge to that at Tarn Hall. A painful suspicion flashed into her mind as she heard Jim's prattle, and recalled the notice which Thornburgh had been taking of Gay. His only half-concealed impatience of Mabel's questioning strengthened the suspicion. Mrs. Fletcher did not like the touch of confusion in his manner, and she liked as little his cousinly lack of ceremony.

He spoke in a very different way to Gay.
His tone to her was absurdly deferential,
and one could not imagine his putting her
queries aside.

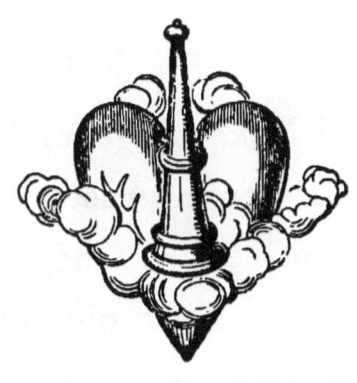

CHAPTER III.

INFORMATION RECEIVED.

" I will tell you a thing, but you shall let it dwell darkly with you."

All's Well that Ends Well.

MR. HELM kept a general shop at the village of St. Austin's, and had a flourishing business. One afternoon in January he was making out bills for some of the gentlefolks who had running accounts with him, and was in a very genial mood, for the sum total of these accounts was highly satisfactory, and he knew that they would be paid as soon as they were sent in. For the present, at any rate, he need entertain no fear of being starved out by those abominable institutions, the stores, which, as a retail dealer, he hated with a perfect hatred.

He was putting up the bills, when a stranger entered the shop. Mr. Helm was well pleased, not only for commercial reasons—he was a sociable man and enjoyed a chat. This person was probably a new-comer to the place (it was not a time of year for stray tourists), and he would have to tell who and what he was, and would naturally desire information, which Mr. Helm would supply in abundance.

The grocer went forward from his desk, and as he regarded his new customer his hope of a little talk collapsed. The man did not invite social advances ; there was something repellent in his lean face and the gloomy eyes, which did not look directly at his interlocutor.

Mr. Helm prepared to serve this person with no superfluous words, and spoke at first only of the goods he was asked for. But, to his surprise, the sullen-looking stranger was by no means taciturn. He soon began talking of other things than business, and gave as full an account of himself as even the curiosity of a village gossip could desire.

His name was Pelter, and he came from New Zealand with a gentleman in whose service he was. This gentleman was named Brown. He was at present in very poor health, and had come to this neighbourhood to try what country quiet and mountain air would do for him. He was in a bad way—here a signifi-cant look aad gesture, which caused Mr.

Helm to nod in full comprehension and say—

" Ay, that's very bad ! And you look after him, I suppose ? "

" Just so," returned Mr. Pelter. " Of course you won't mention it"—lowering his voice. " It's not a thing that one would want to be talked of, you know, especially in a country place like this ; but, between you and me, that's the fact."

" Oh no, no ; of course I won't mention it," protested the grocer. " I'm never one to gossip ; you may be sure that anything is safe with me. And the poor gentleman —is he much of a charge to you ? "

" Well, at times there's a good deal to do with him. He isn't dangerous, but fidgety and troublesome. He's had a peck of trouble—that's at the bottom of it. He's had losses—very heavy losses "

—impressively. (Mr. Helm was respectfully interested, and rapidly decided that he would give no credit to this new customer.) "That's made him melancholy; he is in a very low way."

"I hope he isn't so badly off," said Mr. Helm, sympathetically.

"I fear he is. That's partly what brought him here. He can live cheaper in a country place, and he found he could get a house at a very low rent here."

"What house has he got?"

"Kelvers, they call it — four miles away."

Mr. Helm exclaimed in surprise—

"That lonely place!"

"It's the very place for him. The least excitement upsets him, and he can't bear seeing people since he lost his fortune. He has to be kept as quiet as possible."

" And are you there alone with him ? "

Mr. Pelter replied that he was. His employer objected to seeing strange faces, and he could easily manage all the work required.

" I don't care to have people about the place," he remarked. " They would cackle, and they would make him worse, which would give me more trouble."

" He ought to pay you well for all you do." .

" Well, he makes it worth my while. I don't know that it comes out of his pocket. I fancy some relation of his finds the money ; but, anyway, I *am* paid. And I certainly shouldn't stay with him if it wasn't worth my while," observed Mr. Pelter, emphatically.

Mr. Helm fully believed that. His new acquaintance did not look as if disinterested benevolence were his weakness.

Then the conversation took a turn, and Mr. Helm became the chief speaker. A handbill of one of the concerts which Mr. Ashton had got up was lying on the counter, and Mr. Pelter noticed it and asked a good many questions about the entertainment and the performers. From this the talk naturally flowed to the families of the performers, and the stranger learnt many facts about them and their history.

Mr. Helm was not surprised that his customer stayed a long time. He had a modest assurance that his talk might interest any one, and it must be indeed a treat to a man who lived shut up with a maniac in a lonely house on the moorland.

Mr. Pelter ordered a good many things,

and paid ready money, without receiving any hint that this course would be desirable. When at last he took his departure, he left a very favourable impression behind him.

He walked slowly through the village, and lounged for a time on the bridge over the beck, regarding every passer-by with a keen, furtive glance. He did not see the person he was looking for, and presently he moved on, and took the road that led to Kelvers. It was a dreary afternoon. The sky was grey, and the wind blew from the north with a sullen moaning sound. Pelter shrank together in his great-coat, as he met the bitter gusts, and muttered some angry words between his teeth.

"Such a notion to come to a beastly hole like this! Well, he won't *much* like

to hear what I've got to tell him.
Wonder what he'll do now ? " ·

He passed the gate of Westby Lodge,
and lingered there for a while, as he had
lingered on the bridge.   He heard steps
and voices approaching, and promptly
drew back into the shadow of some trees
that grew just inside the fence of the
grounds, where he could not be seen from
the gate. Gay came up, with Thornburgh
on one side and Jim on the other.   Pelter
saw her face, bright with amusement, and
watched her as she went up the drive ;
then he walked on quickly, with a frown
and shake of the head.

Kelvers stood at some distance from
the highway. It was a small house, which
had been built for a shooting lodge, and
was useless for that purpose now, as its
owner had sold most of his land in the

neighbourhood. But he could not get rid of Kelvers; nobody wanted that, and it had stood empty and half-furnished for long. It was a dreary place, with the bare moorland surrounding it. Not a light gleamed from a window, and the pale blue smoke which rose from the roof had a melancholy look as the wind caught it and flung it about.

Pelter went round to the back. There was a little garden there, shut in by stone walls. Passing through this, he entered the house, and opened the door of one of the front rooms. Here there was light enough. A splendid fire was blazing in the big old-fashioned grate, and a lamp was burning clearly. The closely shuttered and curtained windows allowed nothing of this illumination to be seen without. The furniture was old and scanty, and in great disorder; chairs stood about anywhere, the table was covered with a heterogeneous accumulation of things; but the occupant of the room was evidently making himself comfortable.

He had taken the easiest armchair, and was sitting close to the fire, smoking a good cigar, with a book in his hand. As the door opened, he raised his head with a quick nervous movement. He had a heavy dark moustache and beard, which almost hid the lower part of his face; his eyes were dark and restless, and he had a worn sickly look.

"What a time you've been, Pelter!" he said in a sharp tone.

Pelter said nothing. He crossed the room to the fire and put more coal on.

"Have you done anything? heard anything?"

"Yes," said Pelter, carefully arranging a block of coal ; " I've heard a few things."

" Leave that coal alone, and tell me the ' few things.' You are so slow "—querulously. "What have you found out ? "

" I've found out where the young lady is," replied Pelter, his visage as unmoved by his employer's querulousness as if it had been carved out of wood. "She's living at a Mr. Mildmay's here."

" Oh ! I remember the name. Governess, I suppose. Well, any more ? How about Mrs. Rushton ? Did you hear where she is ? "

" Yes, I heard. She has married Mr. Mildmay."

The other started, and after a pause, laughed.

" The deuce she has ! That's rather awkward ! Married, and to Mildmay——"

He whistled and shrugged his shoulders. "When did it come off, Pelter?—did you hear that? Last October? Good Lord, I never thought of that!"

He sat silent for a minute or two, looking into the fire with a frown.

"Married!" he said again, in a tone of surprise. "Well, that *is* a piece of news! I suppose it was the best thing she could do. Mildmay is well off, I believe. Did you by good luck see anybody?"

"Miss Rushton."

"Did you speak to her?"

"No. Hadn't a chance; she wasn't alone."

"You're such a wooden-headed fellow" —fretfully. "You never have a chance, according to you. Why didn't you make one? You could easily have invented an excuse for speaking to her alone. You must find some way soon of letting her know I am here. I want to see her. Nobody but a fool would have missed her as you did in town. Such a nuisance that was, after I had gone to the trouble of taking rooms near that little actress to be on the watch!"

"I'll manage it as soon as I can," said Pelter. "It won't do to tell her when there are people about; it's sure to give her a start, and you want to lie low here, I understood."

"Yes, I wish to be *incognito* here—you were right, Pelter, in being cautious"—in a tone of good-humoured apology. "I must not be in too great a hurry. By the way, what did you say about me to your informant this afternoon?"

"Just what you told me to say. You've had heavy losses, which has upset you;

you're out of your head, and I'm your keeper; and you've come here because you can't abide seeing folks and must live very cheap."

" You laid it on about my being poor ? "

" I did that."

" You didn't forget to add that this must be kept a secret ? "

" No, I didn't forget that."

" That's a sure way of spreading a story. Tell people that it is not to be talked of, and they can't deny themselves the pleasure of repeating it; what you said will soon be over the village. We shall not be disturbed, Pelter; nobody will want to come near me; they will be afraid that I may ask for a loan. I have made myself secure from intrusion; poverty would be enough of itself to keep people away. If you want to be a hermit, you have only to give out that you are in need ; and the mental derangement adds another safeguard, and prevents people from wondering at my living in this way.".

CHAPTER IV.

"SOME PLEASURES LAST A MONTH."

"Jetzt ist sie da, die kalte Schreckenshand
  Die in mein fröhlich Hoffen schaudernd greift."
                                    Wallenstein.

THAT Christmas and New Year was
a season of special rejoicing for
Sophy. Every day made her surer that
Thornburgh was attracted by Gay, and
she was full of exultant delight in what
she regarded as a brilliant triumph for
her stepdaughter. Gay would carry off
the best match of their set in the neighbourhood, and thereby win golden opinions
which would gild the name of Rushton
handsomely.

In the circle of the Fletchers' acquaint-
ances there were certainly men that were
richer than Thornburgh; but they were
none of them gifted with intellect beyond
the mediocre average. Thornburgh had
a high local reputation for talent and cul-
ture, and was considered very hard to
please. His admiration conferred a distinction which could not be given by men
of lower attainments and less fastidious
taste. Now and then a prophet *has* honour
in his own country; and when that is the
case, he receives much warmer worship
from his neighbours than from the world
at large.

Sophy's joy was so great that it made
her discreet for once, and she kept strict
silence on the subject with Gay. She
did not at all understand Gay, but she
felt sure that hints or jests would offend

her, perhaps make her stiff and cold to Thornburgh, and that would never do.

She confided her hopes and raptures to her husband, who at first was inclined to treat them as delusions, but presently became more respectful, and admitted that Thornburgh *was* very much smitten.

" But, you know, Sophy, it may only be a flirtation. I wouldn't make too sure," he prudently warned her. " It's one thing to have a fancy for a girl, and it's quite another to marry her; and Mabel would be a much better match."

But Sophy indignantly refused to heed this warning. Miles would never excite expectations which he did not mean to fulfil—such a course would be dishonourable, though perhaps most men did not think so. Mr. Mildmay took with perfect equanimity this scathing reflection on his sense of honour.

"The question is whether he means to excite expectations," he observed, "and whether he is exciting them. Gay is no fool; she is 'cute enough to see if a man means business or not."

Argument was not Sophy's *forte*, and her reply was not to the point. She reproved her husband for using such a phrase as "means business"—it sounded so common; and Mr. Mildmay said no more.

The days which brought such joy to Sophy were not so kind to Mrs. Fletcher. That lady, having been roused to observation, saw how the current was setting with Thornburgh, and she did not like it at all. Without having formed definite matchmaking plans, she had cherished a hope that Mabel might become her cousin's wife. It would be so very suitable; everything seemed to mark them out for each other; and she would be so sure of Mabel's prosperity and happiness. It was provoking to see him drawn aside from his proper allegiance by a person of so little consequence as Gay Rushton.

Mrs. Fletcher had a sense of jealousy on her own account, quite apart from Mabel. She had come to look upon Thornburgh as in a way her own property; the man who gave her advice, performed commissions for her, and was generally useful. Their terms of intimacy had been a gratification to her, and it annoyed her to think of Gay's having stronger claims on him.

She could not believe that, if left to

himself, he could really find more charm
in the society of this nobody than in that
of a Fletcher. It was not, she felt assured,
a spontaneous preference. Gay had laid
herself out to please him, and had thus
gained his attention. Mabel was too
simple to understand or make such
efforts. For no consideration would Mrs.
Fletcher have destroyed her daughter's
simplicity, and though she tried to make
her more equal to Gay in power of attraction, her precepts were framed on noble
ideals. It is a woman's duty to be agreeable and give pleasure.

Mabel was not a good pupil. She was
slow in grasping the new lesson. The
idea of pleasing Miles, or entertaining
him, had never entered her head. In intercourse with her, cousin she expected to
take, not to give. He was to listen to

her, to answer her questions, to take an interest in what she told him; his own affairs and interests dwelt in a region of obscurity concerning which she did not think enough to form a conjecture.

"You ought to talk to Miles about himself, Mabel," her mother said, one evening after they had been dining at Westby Lodge. "At dinner you talked of nothing but your own doings, I think, and this parish entertainment. Men are bored by that sort of thing, dear; they like to talk of their own affairs."

"How *can* I talk of Miles's affairs?" asked Mabel, helplessly. "I shouldn't know what to say—I know nothing about them; he doesn't tell me about them."

"You should show him that you would like to hear, and then he would tell you. A woman should be sympathetic and interested in other people. Ask him about his writing."

(Sophy had taken occasion to remark that Miles talked to Gay about his articles, and had read one to her that day in manuscript. "Gay is so clever. She really enjoys that sort of thing," said Sophy, with pride.)

"Oh, mother, I could not! I don't think he would like me to ask questions, and I understand nothing about writing."

"I think he would like your sympathy, dear."

Mabel was sadly at a loss. Interest? Sympathy? She had none at her cousin's service. It was rather unreasonable of Mrs. Fletcher to make such demands on her daughter, for she herself was not at all sympathetic in nature. She had not the quick imagination and the fine

sensitiveness which can readily respond to
another's pains or joys. She could be
very kind ; but sympathy is quite distinct
from kindness, and is a much rarer grace.
You may find five hundred kind people
for one that will comprehend and enter
into your emotions.

But help was at hand for Mrs. Fletcher.
An ally that she knew not of was coming
on the scene.

" By the way," observed Mr. Mildmay,
one morning at breakfast, " Kelvers is let,
I hear."

"That out-of-the way place!" said Sophy,
languidly.   " Who can have taken it ? "

"A philosopher or a hermit, surely,"
remarked Thornburgh, laughing.   " Nobody else could stand the dreariness and
loneliness."

" The new tenant is not quite right,

they say," said Mr. Mildmay. "He is melancholy mad, and has to live in seclusion, and his friends have sent him here with two keepers. He has violent fits at times, in which he is dangerous."

It was two days since Pelter had visited the grocer's shop, and already this account, and others, of the new tenant of Kelvers had been retailed to Mr. Helm, who felt some disgust at finding that his new acquaintance had not made him his sole confidant. The story of the maniac *must* have been told by Mr. Pelter. Mr. Helm had been very careful not to spread it. He had only repeated it to his wife and his brother-in-law as the servant was going in and out of the room, laying the table for supper.

"Oh dear, I hope he will be kept safe," said Sophy, with a little shiver. "It would be very awkward if one met him when one was alone."

"He will be well looked after, no doubt," said Mr. Mildmay, reassuringly. "You hardly ever go out alone, Sophy; you need not be nervous."

"No; but Gay walks out alone a great deal, and she might meet him. Gay, you must not go towards Kelvers; it is such a lonely road. Promise me that you will not go that way."

"I am not in the least afraid of this maniac," said Gay, smiling. "Two keepers will surely be enough to restrain him, dear."

Sophy became plaintive.

"Oh, Gay, you are so foolhardy. Suppose he escaped—madmen are so cunning—and you fell in with him, what *would* you do ?"

"Well, really, I don't know till I am tried what I should do."

"Miss Rushton would quell him with her unflinching gaze," said Thornburgh.

"He might quell her with a stick," said Sophy, prosaically. "Now, Gay, really you must be careful. Please promise not to walk towards Kelvers. It is silly to run unnecessary risks."

"Very well, dear; I won't go that way without your leave. It isn't a pleasant walk at this time of year; it is too muddy."

Gay heard of the strange inhabitant of Kelvers without the faintest suspicion that he was in any way connected with her. She was visited by no dim foreboding that the sword she dreaded was about to fall on her. Fear had ceased to haunt her lately. She was so happy that she could not be afraid of what the future might bring. The storm that had threatened was averted; it *could* not come now. Heaven was merciful and had spared her.

She had resigned herself wholly to the new influences which had come into her life, and no longer made such modest claims on fate. The time had been when she had thought it was enough for her to have food, raiment, and shelter secure, and to be left in· peace; and she believed herself content with these things. But she felt now the pathos of that content. There was so much more in life than she had dreamed of; and she was not one of the disinherited, after all. Joy could come to her, and she stretched out eager, longing arms to welcome it.

"What are you going to do while we are away, Gay?" asked Sophy.

They were going to Castleton on various errands.

"I think I shall go to Tarn Hall to practise with Mabel for the next concert. She is not quite perfect in the accompaniments."

"I don't think Mabel is a good accompanist," observed Mrs. Mildmay.

"Oh, she does very well. She only needs practice. She isn't in the habit of playing accompaniments."

"These entertainments take up a great deal of time," said Thornburgh, disapprovingly. "You give up most of your afternoons to practising now."

"They are for a good object. We ought not to grudge time for that," said Gay, sedately.

She liked to hear Thornburgh grumble at the engagements which lessened the

time she could bestow on him. It was
small-minded, perhaps, but it pleased her
to feel her power over him, even in trifling
matters like this. It was the first time
that her presence had been of so much
importance.

"You won't effect much of the good
object," he frankly told her. "The
audience won't be half so well entertained
by your best singing as by a vulgar comic
song."

"We must try to improve their taste,"
said Gay.

"It's time you all got ready," remarked
Mr. Mildmay. "We must be off in a few
minutes."

Sophy hastily rose, and there was a
little bustle of preparation. Gay came
out to the door to see the party start.
They were in the phaeton, for Mr. Mild-

may had a rooted objection to a close
carriage, and would use one only at night.
Jim, who was going for new garments,
sat between Thornburgh and the groom,
wrapped in the inglorious fur tippet. He
leaned forward to impress upon Gay that
Fido was not to have any sugar during his
absence.

"He wants a beating; you might give
it him," he cheerfully suggested.

Gay laughed, and declined the task.
She stood on the top step, the morning
sunshine falling on her head and shining
in her dark eyes, and waved her hand.
Thornburgh turned to look at her as they
drove away.

She spent the morning in attending to
domestic affairs; she was always diligent
in her care of the housekeeping; and
when she had finished she went out for

a short walk before luncheon. She had
only taken a few steps beyond the gate
when she saw a man coming towards her.
There was something familiar in his
appearance, and she looked more closely
to see who it was, and recognized him.
She had seen that thin dark face—those
deep-set eyes, with their furtive glance—
before. Fate had dogged her, and caught
her up at last.

She stopped short for a moment, turning
white; then she walked on. If she had
been facing the dangerous lunatic Sophy
feared, she could not have set her face
more unflinchingly.

"You wish to speak to me?" she said
quietly to the man.

He gave her the message he had
brought. She was requested to go to
Kelvers as soon as she could; and she

replied that she would go that afternoon.

It was a brilliantly fine afternoon when
Gay started on her walk to Kelvers. The
sun shone, the blue of the sky was dark
and cloudless, the snow on the tops of the
distant mountains glittered and sparkled.

She walked fast, eager to face the worst
and get it over. She did not speculate
about the coming interview, or what might
follow it; she dared not. If she once let
her thoughts rove that way she could not
bear the pain; it would drive her mad.
And she must keep her wits as well as
she could, for she must be strong for
Sophy.

Once a darting thought flashed across
her mind of what this meant for Sophy—
Sophy, who only yesterday had told her,
with tremulous smiles, of a hope that

brightened the future—and she stood still, and wrung her hands in impotent despair.

"Oh, my God! how can she bear it? It must kill her. If only she could die before she knows!"

Gay shuddered. That was the best prayer she could make for the poor foolish, tender soul who had given her most of the affection she had known. She had loved Sophy so well—loved her for her weakness and helplessness, loved her because of the dependence which had braced her to fight the world on her behalf; and it had all come to this, that she would be glad to learn that she was dead.

The path to Kelvers led through a plantation of larches. In this she was met by Pelter.

"I beg pardon, miss," he said awkwardly, "but I'd better tell you that he

doesn't know I saw you in London. I
told him I missed you in the station."

He drew back, giving her no time to
reply, and took a short cut through the
grove. He admitted her when she reached
the house.

She was very pale when she crossed
the threshold; she shrank with uncon-
trollable repugnance from the meeting,
and as Pelter opened the door of the
sitting-room she hesitated for a moment,
then, throwing back her head as if facing
and defying a danger, she entered.

CHAPTER V.

THE TENANT OF KELVERS.

"Il a le tort d'exister; c'est un tort grave."
Samuel Brohl et Cie.

FATHER and daughter stood face to face in silence for a moment. Mr. Rushton did not find himself so much master of the situation as he had expected to be. Gay had become a more formidable person than the young girl he remembered. This stately young woman, with her haughtily held head and stern face, embarrassed him. Gay, on her side, was as much struck with the change years had made in her father. He had aged very much, and he looked out of health. A wave of compassion surged up in her heart. It was piteous that she, the only child of this broken man, cared nothing for him and shrank from him. It was his own fault that it was so; but that only made the sadness of it greater.

"Well, Gay!" said Mr. Rushton, a little impatient of her grave regard.

That rush of softened feeling helped her over the awkwardness of the first greeting. She held out her hand, and when he kissed her she did not draw back.

"Sit down here," he said, pushing an armchair nearer to the fire. "It is very cold this afternoon."

She obeyed. She had come there feeling as if she were going to put herself into the hands of a torturer, and she was invited to a comfortable seat by the hearth. It was as strange and incongruous as a dream.

"I'm glad to see you at last," went on her father, in an even conversational tone; he had overcome his embarrassment now. "I've had plenty of trouble to find you. I saw you in London in October, and supposed you were working there, and wasted time in making inquiries after you. At last I came here, thinking that I might get some clue to your whereabouts through the Fletchers."

"I wonder that you wanted to find me after all these years," said Gay, bitterly.

"I couldn't help leaving you; it was a case of needs must," returned Mr. Rushton, quickly. "I had got myself into such a deuce of a hole that I couldn't possibly stay in England; I was obliged to run away, and I was so badly off that

I couldn't take you and Sophy with me.
It was better for you that I should
vanish. If I had stayed, it would have
been worse for you than it was. You
wouldn't have liked to see me in a police
court."

She made an inarticulate exclamation,
crimsoning hotly with pain and shame.

"Yes," said Mr. Rushton, in grave
lowered tones, "it would have been a
terrible thing for us all, Gay. I couldn't
run that risk."

"But what—what—father, how could
you have been in danger of such a thing?"
she demanded.

This was worse than the worst she had
ever believed or suspected of him.

"*I* had done nothing"—with dignity.
"But I got mixed up in a speculation
with some men, who drew me in so that

I could be made responsible for their doings; and then they decamped, leaving me to bear the brunt. The only safe way for me was to escape. I thought it was best for you that I should leave you; people would be kinder to you if I was a solitary wanderer—they would pity you and help you."

There was a pause. Gay had nothing to say; she could not believe that her father had been innocent in those old transactions, and she was bewildered by his view of the step which had always seemed to her utterly disgraceful and unpardonable. Instead of being bowed to the earth by shame for his desertion of wife and child, he represented it as something for which no blame could attach to him, almost as something meritorious. While she had regarded him as cruelly selfish, he claimed to have considered her good!

And he was quite sincere in his view; she could see that he spoke in good faith, and fully believed in the force of his excuses.

"I had a hard time of it," resumed the solitary wanderer; "I have been through worse difficulties than you have any idea of. I kept silence, for I could do nothing for you, and I would not pain you by telling you what I was brought to. But at last my luck turned—it was about time it did—and I made some money. When I had enough to be of use to you, Gay, I came over to England to find you."

Gay was still silent. She was very much surprised at this announcement, for her father had always been in pecuniary straits in old times, and she regarded him as one that was fast bound by the genius of poverty. It did not rejoice her to hear that he was well-to-do ; for that fact destroyed the only chance that had ever occurred to her of saving Sophy from the misery of learning that she was innocently a bigamist. Mr. Rushton might be willing to leave her in peace for a consideration, which consideration Gay had resolved she would do her utmost to supply. She would find an engagement as a singer, and give him every penny she could spare. She would do better now her voice was so much stronger. It was for that end that she had worked so diligently. But her father's flourishing circumstances put out of the question the bribe she had dreamt of offering.

"I am able now to make up for the troubles we have been through," went on

Mr. Rushton, who apparently laboured under the delusion that he had borne his part in all the privations of his wife and daughter. "We can live in luxury, as you ought to live, Gay."

"We heard more than three years ago that you were dead," said Gay, in a hard tone.

"Ah, that was when I was at the very lowest, and had no hope of ever being better. It was convenient that I should be supposed to have shuffled off this mortal coil, and I made a man write to you that I was dead. I thought it would make no difference to you and Sophy, as things were."

"It has made a great deal of difference to Sophy."

"Yes, indeed! I never thought that that would happen! I was taken aback,

I can tell you, when I found myself
another Enoch Arden. I suppose it was
what I might have expected ; I *didn't*
behave to Sophy as I should "—in a tone
of frank confession. " I know she had a
good deal to complain of. A man as
harassed and bothered as I was could
not be pleasant company at home, and
Sophy at the best of times didn't help
one to. bear one's worries. But she
certainly wasn't a widow long."

A thrill of moral disgust and repulsion
ran through Gay as she listened. Her
father had no pity for Sophy, apparently
no perception of the cruel tragedy of her
position ; his chief feeling seemed to be
mortification and resentment that she had
given him a successor.

" It was three years after the news of
your death came," she said.

Mr. Rushton made as though he had not heard. He chose to regard Sophy's second marriage as disrespectful in its haste to the memory of her first husband, and a fact which did away with that theory he preferred to ignore.

"Poor Sophy!" sighed Gay.

"Eh? Isn't she comfortable now? Has Mildmay his little faults like other men?"—with a laugh.

Gay looked at him with horror at this levity; it seemed brutal just then.

"Oh, father, how can you? She will die when she knows that—that——"

"Knows what? That I am still in the flesh? But how should she know?"

"You don't mean to tell her?" cried Gay, breathlessly.

"Not I," said Mr. Rushton. "No, indeed"—more emphatically. "I can't

flatter myself that my reappearance would
be hailed with welcome, and I'll leave her
to Mildmay. They have my blessing.
I'll remain the dear departed. She need
not hear of me, provided you hold your
tongue, and I know you could always
do that. Why "—breaking off abruptly—
" what is the matter ? "

Gay was sobbing in the sudden relief
from her tormenting fear.

" I am so glad that you will leave her in
peace," she said between her sobs. " I
was so afraid—it would be so awful for
her to find out——"

" That she isn't married at present ? "
said Mr. Rushton, in a tone which sent
that thrill of repulsion again through his
daughter. " Yes, that would be very
awkward for her. But it would do me no
good to make my existence known to her.

We could scarcely live together after this interlude. I never thought of telling her after I heard that she had changed her name. You may be quite at ease, Gay. It is rather hard on a man," he added, in a mournful tone, "after being battered and knocked about the world as I have been, to find himself in such a position, alone and homeless. But it can't last much longer, and a few more years will make little difference."

Gay was utterly unmoved by this last touch, which she regarded as merely a rhetorical flourish.

"I don't want to disturb anybody. As you have done so well without me, I can go my own way again in silence. Of course it is the common lot—a man is forgotten at once; his place is filled up directly."

Mr. Rushton's tone was a masterly blending of lofty pity for poor human nature and patient magnanimity for its frailty. Apparently his solitary wanderings had a little affected his memory, for he spoke as though his recent seclusion had been brought about by his wife and daughter.

Gay was fully aware of the flagrant injustice of this bold assumption that he was an injured man, and her sense of humour was touched by his complaint that they had forgotten him. And yet she was sorry for him. It was hard to find one's self overlived and superfluous. Perhaps he really wished to make atonement for past neglect, and it must be bitter to have no place for repentance.

"Father, we could not help it," she said deprecatingly.

" Ah, well, it's no good talking of it."

Mr. Rushton dismissed the subject, and began talking of his life since he had left England. He had much to tell of his travels and experiences, and he held forth with the keen relish of an egotist who has a new and attentive auditor.

" What made you come here ? " asked Gay, presently.

" I told you why. I wanted to find out what had become of you and Sophy, and this was the place where information seemed most attainable. Of course you applied to the Fletchers when I had gone, and they did something for you."

" But why did you come to this house, father ? It is so dreary and lonely."

" Oh, the house does well enough. I prefer a quiet, out-of-the-way place at present. If I had gone to the village, there would have been no end of gossip about me, and I wished to avoid that. In fact"—in a slightly irritable tone—"seclusion at this juncture is convenient for me. You needn't look startled ; it is nothing serious."

"You live here alone with that man ? "

"Yes ; nobody else comes about the place, and he is quite to be trusted. He won't let anything out, so you need not have any fears. He is a good fellow in his way. I picked him up in America—saved his life when he was very ill, and he has been with me ever since. He is devoted to me."

Gay reflected that the man could have no motive for betraying his employer's secrets, and good reasons of self-interest for keeping strict silence about them.

The security for his discretion was strong enough. She longed to ask one more question, and to be assured that her father was going to take his departure at once, but she felt it difficult to bring out the words. It seemed unfeeling to show too plainly her eagerness to be rid of his presence in the neighbourhood.

The fading of the light warned her that she ought to start on her walk back.

" I must be going," she said. " It is rather a long way to Westby Lodge."

" Must you go ? When can you come again ? I suppose you can manage to pay me a visit occasionally ? "

Her heart sank, partly at the intimation that her parent intended to remain for some time, partly at the thought of those future visits. They would be much more difficult and dangerous than Mr. Rushton seemed to imagine.

"I will come when I can," she said; "but I cannot always command my time."

"Oh, you can't be such a slave that you can't find an hour now and then for your father"—in tones of gentle remonstrance.

It would be useless to point out that a visit to Kelvers took more than an hour; the walk there and back filled up two. Mr. Rushton's idea of parental claims evidently excluded all consideration of such small practical details.

"I will come when I can," repeated Gay. "How long shall you be here?" she added abruptly.

"I don't exactly know. I haven't decided. When can you manage to slip away again ?" persisted Mr. Rushton. " This week ? "

" Oh no, impossible ! Perhaps I could come next Monday."

" All right ; I shall expect you then."

CHAPTER VI.

STRATEGY.

"Um ihrer Ruhe willen muss es ihr
Verschwiegen bleiben.
            Warum überall
Auch das Geheimniss?"

Wallenstein.

NO man, it has been said, can jump off his own shadow. It is a sadder truth, in many cases, that a man's relations cannot jump off his shadow. When he comes between them and the sun, they must bear the chill and darkness which he throws over them; by no effort can they shake themselves free of him.

Mr. Rushton's shadow had completely

blotted out all the brightness of his
daughter's life that afternoon, and Gay's
heart was very heavy as she walked
slowly back, pondering the situation.
She had been freed from the great anxiety
which tormented her, and she told herself that to have Sophy left in peace was
so great a good that she ought to care
for nothing else. But relief on Sophy's
account would not swallow up every other
sensation, and the dismissal of that black
care only made room for the consideration
of Gay's strictly personal share of trouble.

As she went, she recalled the conversation, and the bitter feeling it had stirred
within her surged up again. Separation
and absence had somewhat softened down
her father in her remembrance, and, since
she had believed him to be dead, she
had thought of him less severely, and had

tried to make excuses for his many defects. But her father alive was a person concerning whose moral worth nobody could cherish any fond illusions. He had revolted her unutterably by his selfishness, his egotism, his pity for himself, and his callous indifference to the consequences that his desertion of wife and child might have caused.

She was angry with him for the frankness which he had shown. Why had he told her the disgraceful reason of his flight from England? He might have refrained from that confidence and left her a shred of respect for him. But he did not even understand how his confession affected her. He was utterly lacking in moral perception.

The shame which he could not feel for himself Gay felt so deeply that there was a sense of unfitness upon her as she considered the chief effect which his untimely reappearance would have on her life. What possible tie could there be between her father's daughter and Miles Thornburgh? She had no right to think of him as anything but an acquaintance; she ought never to have let herself dream of more. She must give up her dreams— ah, there was nothing to give up. If he knew what she knew, he would turn away from her.

"I might have known it would come to this," she told herself. "I *did* know; but I shut my eyes, and would not acknowledge that I saw the end plainly. Of course I couldn't be so happy. It was preposterous to imagine that such a wild impossibility could come to pass. Well, I am shown my proper place again, and I will take it. I *won't* be sentimental, and make a fuss, and think I am very unhappy. I have been a little mad, and fancied I had a chance of drawing a big prize; but now I am quite sane, and I won't break my heart for a fancy. After all, what do I lose? Only what I ought never to have had—what I should never have had a chance of if the whole truth had been known."

And the rest of the walk was spent in meditating on the best way of breaking off the intimacy which had grown up between her and Thornburgh. It must be done at once, and it did not appear an easy task.

But she received unexpected help from Jim. That youth had enjoyed himself very much at Castleton, for Sophy had let him do just as he pleased, and he had thrown off the tippet, and eaten a heavy lunch at a confectioner's. Exposure to cold and excesses in pastry laid him low, and for a few days he needed a good deal of attention; and Gay spent most of her time with him, glad of such an unassailable reason for seclusion.

After a day or two in his own room, Jim was allowed to go to the schoolroom for change of scene. Gay sat there one afternoon, holding him on her knee and telling him stories, when Thornburgh came in.

"Sophy gave me leave to pay Jim a visit," he said. "How are you, old fellow?"

"I have a very bad cold," replied Jim, with melancholy dignity.

"You are quite a prisoner with him, Miss Rushton—one sees nothing of you. Don't you get very tired?"

"Poor Jim must be nursed," said Gay.

Thornburgh knelt down on the rug, and looked at her as she sat with the firelight full on her face.

"It is awfully dull without you," he said, in a tone of complaint. "Shall you be visible this evening?"

"I think not. The nurse will be out, and I don't like to leave Jim."

"But, good heavens, he isn't dangerously ill! Put him to bed, and come down to dinner."

"He wouldn't like that. Would you, Jim?"

"No," said Jim, decidedly.

"You make a slave of yourself to the child," said Thornburgh. "It is quite unnecessary, and it is very bad for him."

"I like to look after him," protested Gay; "and I really can't very well leave him to-night. He is feverish and restless in the evening."

"Come and sit on my knee a little while, Jim," said Thornburgh, "and let Miss Rushton rest."

But Jim was very comfortable where he was, and disinclined to move, and Gay declared that she did not need any rest.

Thornburgh did not feel encouraged to remain, and he departed with a puzzled scrutinizing glance at Gay. He had come to have a talk with her, and he resented being disappointed. She did not meet the glance; but she felt it, as she had felt every look he had given her since he came into the room, and when he shut the door behind him, she drew a long quivering breath, as though a pain had stabbed her. It was very hard to send him away.

When Monday came she found it possible to pay the visit which she had conditionally promised to her father. Jim was quite well, and Sophy drove out with her husband, so that Gay was free to follow her own devices. She was glad to have her way made smooth, for unwillingly as she went to Kelvers, she had dreaded that she might be prevented from going.

Her father wished to see her, and his wish must be gratified. He had never been a person that it was safe to thwart, for one could not tell what rash impulse might seize him in a fit of irritation; and now, when he held such awful power in his hands, to cross him would be like striking matches in a powder magazine. At any possible cost he must be humoured and kept quiet.

She found her parent in a gloomy mood, and had to hear a long jeremiad. Mr. Rushton drew a moving picture of himself as a victim of "outrageous Fortune," and lamented his hard case, complaining of ill health and of his loneliness. Gay listened patiently, and answered him as soothingly as she could, and her attentions had a good effect. Mr. Rushton brightened up, and became quite cheerful after a while. He ceased to talk of his certainty that his troubles would soon be at an end, and told her that he intended to visit Monte Carlo in the spring.

When Gay rose to go, he was highly amused at the precautions she took against being recognized.

"You are quite romantically disguised," he said; "that thick veil covers your face completely, and that big cloak hides your figure.   Is it necessary?"

"It is better to be careful.   I don't want to have any awkward questions to answer."

"Well, you won't meet anybody near this house; nobody ever comes this way."

He went to the door with her, and detained her in talk for a few moments. At last he said good-bye, and she struck across the moorland.   She had only gone a few steps, when, glancing to the left, she saw two men descending a long slope at right angles to the line she was taking.   They were at some distance, but she knew them at once, and her heart stood still with horror as she recognized Thornburgh and Mr. Ashton.

They must have seen her at the door of the house before she drew down her veil. She would have plenty of awkward questions to answer after this!

In her first alarm she was inclined to retreat to the house to avoid a meeting with them, but quickly coming second thoughts suggested a better way of escape. She did not look again towards the two men, and walked on fast, bearing away sharply to the right, and taking a direction which led to the village, not to Westby Lodge. Presently she came to a plantation, and as soon as she had left the open moorland behind, and knew that she was sheltered from observation, she ran at her best speed. She had been obliged to take a long circuitous route, and she must hurry.

She flew across fields, climbing walls or scrambling through gaps in hedges, pondering the while how she was to prevent any untoward discovery through the unlucky encounter of that afternoon. There was only one plan that she could think of. It was a hateful thing to do, but it was necessary for Sophy's peace, and Gay would not hesitate at any sacrifice or effort for that end.

A servant was crossing the hall as she entered Westby Lodge.

"Is Mrs. Mildmay alone?"

"Yes, ma'am; the master went out again, and Mr. Thornburgh has not come in yet."

So far, so good. Gay had won the first move in the game she had to play. She hurried off her walking gear, joined Sophy in the drawing-room, and rang for tea.

A few minutes later Thornburgh came in, accompanied by Mr. Ashton, who wished to consult Miss Rushton about the next parish entertainment. The curate looked a little surprised at seeing Gay sitting by the fire.

"You have got back very quickly, Miss Rushton," he remarked, when the first greetings were over. "You were driven part of the way, I suppose?"

She looked at him, with a shade of wonder in her expression.

"I got back some time ago," she said serenely. "But I don't understand. Why do you think I was driven?"

"We saw you this afternoon as we were walking over Kelvers Bank, and I thought you could not have walked back so soon."

Gay's expression of wonder deepened, and she looked quite at a loss, as she glanced from Mr. Ashton to Thornburgh. It was very well done; she had never profited so much by her training in acting as she did then.

"You saw me?" she repeated. "Oh, Mr. Ashton, you made a mistake—I was not there."

She told the falsehood carelessly, without undue emphasis. She was only correcting a blunder, not making a statement of any importance; and as she spoke, she met the eyes of each man in turn with an unembarrassed smile.

Mr. Ashton looked bewildered.

"I felt quite sure it was you," he said.

"It certainly was not," said Gay. "I haven't been near Kelvers to-day."

"Indeed, I should hope not," put in Sophy. "It really isn't safe for a lady to go near that house at present."

"Mr. Ashton must have taken somebody else for me," said Gay.

"Yes," said Thornburgh; "it was easy to make a mistake—it has been a dark afternoon, and we were a long way off the figure which we fancied was yours, Miss Rushton."

Mr. Ashton agreed that it had been rash to think he recognized anybody under such circumstances, and plunged into the subject of the next penny reading. Gay listened and talked and laughed, and all the time fear possessed her.

Her falsehood had been successful with Mr. Ashton, but had it been accepted by Thornburgh? Though he had come to her help and supported the lie, she fancied that he knew it was a lie; and she was afraid, not that her secret might be discovered through him—she was quite sure that he would keep silence about that afternoon—but of his loss of respect for her.

She lónged to know what he thought, but she dared not look at him; all her audacity had spent itself for the time, and she shrank and trembled before him.

He did not join in the chat that was going on, and her heart sank lower and lower, as he sat silent. Presently, making a great effort, she turned to him and pointedly addressed him.

"Mr. Ashton wants me to sing an operatic air, and I think a popular sentimental song would be better. What do you think, Mr. Thornburgh?"

"I incline to Mr. Ashton's opinion. You have special gifts for dramatic art, Miss Rushton; it is a pity not to put them to use."

Gay turned away; she had read her condemnation in his face before his words assured her of it.

"Exactly," said Mr. Ashton. "Plenty of people can sing the commonplace sentimental song, but nobody about here can sing anything requiring dramatic expression as Miss Rushton can."

"Nobody," said Thornburgh, emphatically. "It is a rare gift."

"Pray, don't overwhelm me with compliments," said Gay, laughing lightly. "Very well, I will do as you wish, Mr. Ashton."

Thornburgh was taciturn and abstracted at dinner that evening, and avoided talking to Gay afterwards. This passed unnoticed, for Mr. Ashton had been invited to dine, and Gay devoted herself to his special entertainment.

"It is a good thing," she thought drearily, as she smiled and chatted. "I shall have no further difficulty in being less friendly with him ; he is too much disgusted to care to have anything more to do with me. This will make as decided a break as I could wish—it is all over now."

Next day she was arranging flowers in the dining-room, when Thornburgh came in. He said he had come to look for the *Times ;* but this was plainly a pretext, for when Gay informed him that the paper was in the drawing-room, he did not go in search of it. He made a few remarks about the weather, to which she responded quietly, and then there was a pause.

She went on clipping the stalks of the white chrysanthemums and disposing them among ivy leaves, carefully avoiding looking at him. His manner told her the purpose with which he had sought her.

He was not going to drop her in silence and disgust; he wanted an explanation of yesterday, and he had come to give her an opportunity of offering that explanation.

It touched her inexpressibly that he should think it possible for her to make any excuse. She must indeed be dear to him, she thought, with a throb of pride, if he could believe in her so far against appearances; and for one wild moment she longed to tell him the whole truth. It would be such a relief if he understood and thought kindly of her.

But no, it was impossible; she resisted the impulse as if it had been a temptation. The secret she had to keep was not her own; she did not know what harm might be wrought if she let it pass out of her own keeping, what the consequences might

be to her father. Mr. Rushton had not
been explicit about his present position ;
but it was clear to her that his chief
reason for coming to Kelvers had been
that it was expedient for him to keep in
strict retirement. Her ignorance as to
his circumstances made her more cautious.
If Thornburgh knew anything of him,
he might unwittingly bring about the
discovery of his hiding-place. He would
not do it voluntarily, but when one was
utterly in the dark, there was no telling
what danger one might stumble against.

And it was not fair to Thornburgh
himself to tell him. To know of Mr.
Rushton's existence and whereabouts
would only cause him embarrassment ; it
would be selfish and inconsiderate to lay
the 'burden of such a secret on his
shoulders. Gay had always had to stand

alone and carry her burdens herself, not dividing the weight with another ; and to bear this in reticent self-reliance seemed quite simple and natural. Indeed, as she reflected, she felt that it would be easier to do so ; it would be too painful to confide to Thornburgh the facts which had made both her ears tingle.

But there was something else that she wished to say to him. It had struck her that there would be danger in letting the matter rest as it stood. He might think it necessary to make inquiries about the inhabitant of Kelvers, and, with the best intentions, set a match to a train that would explode the mine which Mr. Rushton had prepared. That must be prevented.

" Mr. Thornburgh," she said, turning sideways in her chair towards him, " you know that I told a lie yesterday ? "

She spoke curtly and abruptly, purposely adopting the plainest form of words.

"If anybody but you had told me so, I should have said it was impossible," he returned.

She coloured and paused for a moment; his cold, stern disapproval was hard to face. Then she forced a laugh, a laugh that she had learnt for the stage, and said in a light tone—

"Oh, surely it wasn't such a very dreadful thing! I was obliged to fib, because I did not wish Sophy to hear I had been at that house. The fact is, I knew the tenant some time ago, and he—isn't an acquaintance to be proud of. It would annoy Mr. Mildmay if people connected him with anybody in his family, and so I thought it better to be silent and save Sophy trouble."

Thornburgh's gravity did not relax in the least ; it rather deepened as she spoke.

" I supposed that that was the case," he said. " But, if this person is so objection- able, is it advisable for you to have any- thing to do with him ? "

" I can't very well help it. If I didn't he might annoy Sophy, and I won't have that."

" But how could he annoy Sophy ? Mildmay is quite equal to protecting her from unwelcome visitors."

"Can't you understand that she would dislike very much to see such a person even once, and to be reminded of old times ? It would make her quite unhappy if Mr. Mildmay knew that she had such an acquaintance, and she would hate to think of the man's gossiping about the life we used to lead."

" I do not see how that is to be prevented in any case," said Thornburgh,
stiffly.

" Oh yes, it can be prevented if I keep
him in good humour," rejoined Gay, in a
tone of careless confidence.

" I think you are wrong," said Thornburgh, after a pause. " An acquaintance
that you can only keep up secretly is not
a proper one for you."

" Why not ? I am not a child, and I
am not obliged to give an account of all
my goings and comings to any one."

" But—forgive me—don't you understand that these clandestine visits may
bring you into embarrassment ? "

She understood well enough what he
hinted at, and for a moment hot scarlet
rose in her cheeks, and she drew herself
up in proud anger. Then resentment was

swept away by gratitude: it was very good of him to dare to warn her and try to protect her, even at the risk of affronting her. It was an effort to keep up the flippant tone which she had assumed.

"Oh yes," she said, laughing, "I know that by experience. I got into an awkward fix yesterday; but I got out of it very well. Mr. Ashton *did* believe me" —half-questioning, half-asserting.

"Oh yes, he believed you. He did not see you come out of the house," added Thornburgh. "He did not connect you in any way with that."

"That was a piece of good luck! I shall trust to my wits to extricate me, if I get into a fresh difficulty," she said calmly.

Thornburgh felt intensely disgusted, as well he might, and he was at no pains to keep his disgust out of his expression.

"I am sorry I offered you any suggestion on the subject, Miss Rushton," he said. "It was indiscreet, for I have no right to give you advice."

"Well, I think advice on this matter, however good, is wasted on me," returned Gay. "I should not like to drop a person I knew in our bad times because I am better off now. And it is not only for such noble reasons that I go to Kelvers. I am a Bohemian at heart, and I like to see a fellow-countryman and talk to him. It is quite refreshing after the very proper society I have here."

Thornburgh walked out of the room without a word or glance in reply.

CHAPTER VII.

" MY HEART SHALL BE MY OWN."

"Out went my heart's new fire and left it cold."
R. BROWNING.

IKE Naaman of old, Thornburgh
went away in a rage. He was
angry with Gay because she had ruthlessly
shattered his ideal of her, but he was more
angry with himself for his folly in idealizing
her. He deserved to be written down a
simpleton for his utter failure to read her
character and understand her nature. He
had believed her everything that was
good and true; he had given her the
worship which a high-minded man offers

to the woman he loves; and now she suddenly showed herself the very opposite of what he had imagined her to be.

It had given him a sharp shock when she denied having been at Kelvers. He could not believe her; he had seen her too distinctly to doubt the evidence of his own eyes, and her lie horrified him. It was not only the lie, but the cool, composed way in which she told it, that filled him with disgust. She was evidently prepared for it; and vague fears crept into his mind about the acquaintance which had to be concealed so carefully. Then his heart pleaded against his first stern condemnation, and urged that she might have excuses, and if he knew all he might not blame her so much. He longed to think better of her, and half despised himself for the longing, for hitherto he had regarded falsehood as an unpardonable offence, which destroyed esteem.

He had seen her, and the interview had only made matters worse. Her manner was against her. He could see that she was not speaking openly and frankly; she looked as if she was considering what she should say. She had no excuse to offer that was valid in his eyes. He gave no weight to her desire to protect Sophy from annoyance; no such annoyance as she professed to fear justified her untruth.

That part of her explanation seemed to him a very poor pretence, exasperating in its utter futility. He had only believed her at the last, when she said that she kept up this old Bohemian acquaintance for her own pleasure. He accepted that statement without hesitation.

Gay's strategy had been entirely successful. She had seen that the surest way of keeping her secret was to guard against Thornburgh's divining that there was any secret of importance in question; and so she had represented her reasons for going to Kelvers as inadequate, even frivolous. She had carefully thought out all she should say, and had planned that the confession that she went to enjoy a little Bohemian society should come last; " because," she reflected, " he will be more disposed to believe it, if it seems to be . made unwillingly."

Thornburgh fulfilled her expectations. It was not likely that he should suspect her of inventing a reason for her conduct which did her so little credit. It was impossible to struggle to keep his faith in her after that; the Gay he had believed in did not exist, had never existed. He had been ridiculously deceived by this girl who could lie in sheer levity, and flippantly acknowledge that she preferred keeping up a disreputable acquaintance to deserving his respect.

Thornburgh walked a long way that afternoon, and did not return till just in time to dress for dinner. At that meal he announced that he found it necessary to run up to town to-morrow. Sophy professed regret at losing him so suddenly, and Mr. Mildmay echoed her sentiments in more moderate terms ; but their remarks were lost on the person to whom they were addressed. He was looking at Gay to see how she took his departure. He saw a look of relief on her face, and he was as much stung that she should be glad to get rid of him as if her feelings were of any consequence to him.

"But you aren't going to town for good, surely, Miles?" cried Sophy. "You have a lot of engagements here, I know."

"No, I shall only be away a few days. I must come back again."

. "We shall see you again, then," said Sophy, smiling with recovered cheerfulness.

Thornburgh replied that he would go to his own house, as his housekeeper was well now, and he declined Sophy's invitation to return to them. He would be very busy when he came back, and he could work best when he was alone. Sophy saw that he was decided, and did not press her hospitalities upon him. When she and Gay had left the table, she grumbled at his departure.

"It is strange that he should rush off at a day's notice. Did he say anything about it to you, Gay?"

" No."

Sophy looked sharply at her step-daughter.

" He hasn't proposed to you ? Surely you haven't refused him, Gay ? " — in accents of alarm. " You would never be so silly — why, it would be positively wicked. I am your only relation, and if you get an offer, I ought to know."

Gay turned red, then white ; but she met Sophy's gaze composedly.

" You are quite on the wrong tack with Mr. Thornburgh, dear. He has not made me an offer, and he certainly never will make me one. Pray, put such fancies out of your head ; he doesn't think of me in that way."

Sophy was bewildered at this sudden turn of affairs, but something in Gay's manner imposed silence upon her, and prevented her from lamenting aloud over the ruin of the pretty air-castle she had been so diligently building and furnishing lately.

Thornburgh very soon returned. He did not intend to keep at a distance from Gay ; such a course of action belonged to the usual business of a disappointed lover's part, and that was a character which he altogether declined to assume. He was angrily bent on proving first to himself, and next to Gay and his relations, that his peace of mind was unshaken.

In a few days he was at his own house, keeping his engagements, and going as often as seemed natural to Westby Lodge. He met Gay with unruffled calm, and was ready and friendly in talk with her. But through all his show of friendliness Gay

was as well aware that he had changed
entirely towards her, as she would have
been if he had treated her with marked
neglect. She need give herself no more
trouble to break off their intimacy; that
was done; and, on the whole, she was glad
that it was so. It lessened the strain
upon her, when she had not to avoid
him; and her strength was sufficiently
taxed by the burden of her secret, which
pressed more and more heavily upon
her.

Each day that Mr. Rushton remained
in the neighbourhood added to the danger
of discovery, but apparently it did not
occur to him that he should go quickly.
If Gay hinted an inquiry about his departure, he answered vaguely, fixing no particular time for it. She dared not say
much on the subject, lest her too evident

willingness to part from him should irritate
the spirit of opposition, which was strong
in him, and prolong his stay; she must
wait for a decision which she was powerless to influence.

She was not troubled only by the fear
that some one might discover her father.
It was quite possible that Mr. Rushton
might not be able to refrain from the
pleasure of revealing his existence to
Sophy. The part of Enoch Arden is
strikingly pathetic and effective, and gives
an opportunity for highly emotional scenes,
and Mr. Rushton loved emotional scenes.

He had a craving for mental stimulants
which made excitement of any kind
delightful to him, and his restless vanity
made him desire to be *en évidence*, and to
impress himself upon other people. He
had the sort of temperament that would

prefer the dock or the pillory to absolute
obscurity. It is such men that accuse
themselves of murders they have never
committed.   Half at least of the disasters
of Mr. Rushton's chequered professional
career were caused by these deplorable
idiosyncrasies, for they were always leading him into quarrels. Something offended
his susceptible vanity, and to assert himself
he would rush into a fray, thirsting for
the joys of verbal contest, written or oral.
He generally carried off the honours of
the engagement, for he had a fine flow of
words, and no scruple as to saying in-
sulting things ; but these victories had all
been too like those of Pyrrhus.

When Gay was quite a child,
she had discerned these characteristics.
" Father loves a fuss. Father loves to
show off."   Those had been very early

judgments of hers, for circumstances had
made her mournfully precocious. Now
she lived in constant dread that he might
be unable to resist the temptation of
indulging these weaknesses in the thorough
way that was open to him. He would
not be kept back by fears on his own
account; he would reckon on the silence
of the Mildmays. He was so morally
obtuse that he would suppose they would
have no difficulty in hushing the matter
up, and that the only result of his reappearance would be some very agreeable
excitement for himself.

These anxieties often left little room in
her mind for Thornburgh; and she treated
him with a quiet equanimity, which looked
like indifference, and which irritated him
inexpressibly. This was unreasonable, for
he had persuaded himself that he cared

nothing for her, and therefore it could not matter that she cared nothing for him. But "therefore" is not a word used in the *Pays de Tendre*, and her preoccupied manner increased his bitterness against her. Not only was she frivolous and untruthful, she could never have had any affection for him, and she had merely appeared to like him, no doubt to draw him on for her amusement. And this— alas for his claims to be a stern moralist!— was a heavier count in his indictment against her than her deceit.

He did not give place to such thoughts. He was deeply disgusted at the episode of his fancy for Gay—in that way he described it—and he did all he could to put her out of his head. He stuck close to his work, and he cultivated the society of his neighbours more than usual. In

particular, he went oftener to Tarn Hall.
It was the place which was most nearly
a home to him, and the affection he had
always received there seemed very attrac-
tive in his present humour.

Mrs. Fletcher saw her opportunity, and
for the first time in her life displayed
some ability for management. She petted
him in an unobtrusive way, which he found
very soothing, and she made Mabel share
in her attentions. The girl had learnt
something from the maternal teaching she
had lately received, and she made herself
much more amiable than Thornburgh had
ever known her before.

He felt remorsefully that he had
somewhat neglected these sweet kins-
women, and he gladly returned for more
of the same treatment. Family affection,
based on thorough knowledge, and built

up by years of mutual good offices, was a far more satisfactory thing than a passing love fit. Here he could make no disconcerting discoveries ; here he was sure of his ground. He was just in the mood to be captivated by a new attraction, and it soon struck him that Mabel was very pretty, and that it was pleasant to see her clear blue eyes raised with a look of serious attention while he talked. He hailed the discovery with joy. To fall in love with somebody else would be the most effectual way of forgetting his recent unlucky experiment. Mabel would be an ideally fit wife for him, and he set about bestowing his affections on her.

Meanwhile, Sophy was suffering grievously from disappointment at the downfall of her hopes. Mr. Mildmay had to hear much bitter invective against

men's fickleness, and much abuse of
Thornburgh, and his defence of his cousin
was quite in vain. Sophy persisted in
maintaining that Miles had behaved
shamefully, and required that her husband
should share her indignation. Mr. Mildmay at last declared roundly that he
would not show any coldness to Miles if
he had flirted with a hundred girls. No
such trifles could affect their friendship.

" I believe it is partly Gay's own fault
that he has cooled off," he added. " She
has not seemed very friendly to him
lately, and she has been pleasanter to
Ashton. She has plenty to say to him
about these concerts. She is a little
capricious, I fancy, and Miles wouldn't
stand that sort of thing if he had serious
intentions. But I doubt it. I always
warned you not to expect too much.

He must prefer Mabel. No man would look at Gay if Mabel was by."

"Oh, James, what an unkind thing to say! I thought you liked Gay."

"So I do, dear, very much. I think she is an admirable person in the house. She is a valuable help to you and very kind to Jim, and she sings charmingly. But if I were a young man looking out for a wife, Mabel would be my choice. She is more like you, you see. Perhaps that prejudices me."

This neat compliment raised a smile on Sophy's face, but a heavy sigh followed.

"I wish that Miles's taste was different," she said. "It is so particularly trying that he should change now, before the party at the castle. I quite looked forward to it. I thought Gay would have a success with him in her train, and it would have been a triumph to show that she could make such a conquest. I ordered the prettiest frock for her, and now it has all come to nothing."

The party in question was an entertainment which was given every year by the great man of the district to his country neighbours, and was the chief festivity of the winter.

"But, my dear," mildly suggested the husband, "Gay may be a success without Miles."

"Oh, you know quite well that it won't be so good. To catch Miles is the greatest triumph that a girl here could have. People think him so hard to please. Everybody would have admired her because he did. It is really hard that Mabel should get what I wanted for Gay."

CHAPTER VIII.

A NEW LIGHT.

" I am not made of such slight elements."
Idylls of the King.

EBRUARY passed slowly away.
Fortunately, it was very dry and
fine for the time of year, and the weather
put no difficulty in the way of the stolen
visits to Kelvers. These were as frequent
as Gay could make them, more frequent,
she feared, than was at all prudent; but
they were too few to satisfy her father.

Mr. Rushton was very dull in the place
of abode he had fixed upon. Gay's society

was the only change he could enjoy ; and he constantly required her presence. He wanted her, and it had been the simple rule of his life that he should have what he wanted, if it could possibly be obtained.

He never reflected that his demands were not easily complied with, and that he was selfish in pressing them ; so far from taking that view, he had a pleasant consciousness of virtue in desiring his daughter's company. He had been accustomed to consider domestic intercourse as a matter of duty, not of pleasure, for the male members of a family ; and when he had allowed himself to brighten the hearth of his home, he had complacently felt that he was very good, and that his womenkind were enjoying a great treat. This habit of thought still con-

tinued, and when he told Gay to come
again, he, in all good faith, supposed that
she must be gratified at having so many
opportunities of basking in the paternal
smile. He remembered how in old times
her mother had rejoiced to keep him at
home, how Sophy had complained of his
leaving her to solitude, and he did not
consider that his position was rather
different now.

The dance at the castle was later than
usual that winter, and did not take place
till the end of February. On the day
fixed for it, Thornburgh was at Tarn Hall
in the afternoon. Mabel was unusually
lively in anticipation of the evening, and
thanked him very prettily for some flowers
which he had ordered to be sent her from
London. Mrs. Fletcher was gently
cordial, and he lingered in the firelit

drawing-room which had somehow become such a pleasant place lately.

When he went away Mrs. Fletcher felt with satisfaction that things were going well. He was plainly more and more attracted by Mabel. He had asked her to promise him several dances, and she by some stroke of good luck had been well-advised enough not to grant him all he wanted. "Oh no, she could not promise him more than two now; it would not do to fix so many beforehand," she had said, not at all coquettishly, but with serious serenity. The manner of her denial was even better than the denial itself, and Mrs. Fletcher rejoiced to see her daughter show so much tact. It was better policy to be a little reserved. It would do Miles good; if there was any fault to be found with his behaviour, it was that he was rather too easy and fraternal. If Mabel held aloof, it would teach him more deference and make him more eager.

Thornburgh walked home in the mood of content which the society of the Fletchers had produced in him, thinking of Mabel and the dance, which last would really not be so great a bore as he had found such festivities so far; indeed, it would be pleasant with his pretty cousin, "provided she dances often enough with me," he reflected, smiling. He was not afraid that he should be disappointed when he asked again; he was not accustomed to being crossed by the Fletchers.

There was a way through the grounds of Westby Lodge which made a very convenient short cut to Thornburgh Hall, and which Thornburgh often took. He turned into it this afternoon, and was

walking along a path bounded by a high
hedge of holly, when on the other side of
the trees he heard a familiar voice say in
a low, hurried tone—

"Yes, I will come; tell him so, but——"

The rest was lost.

There was a mutter in a man's voice;
gruff, almost angry, it sounded.

"Tell him I cannot manage it sooner,"
in deprecating accents.

Thornburgh quickened his steps that
Gay might not meet him, but as he
rounded a turn he came upon her hurry-
ing back to the house at her best pace,
and she nearly ran against him.

"I beg your pardon," he said stiffly.
"I was making haste away. I feared I
might interrupt one of the housemaids in
a flirtation."

He was ashamed of the words as soon

as he had uttered them, but he had spoken out of an impulse of ungovernable irritation. The placid calm which he had been enjoying was driven away. It was unbearable that she should act with such want of dignity, and expose herself to rudeness from that low fellow.

She did not appear to comprehend the affront his speech conveyed.

"It is very cloudy and dark," she said, in a quiet, almost absent tone, as if she was thinking of something else.

This indifference to his judgment did not soothe Thornburgh. It was exasperating to see that she was unimpressed while he was so disturbed.

"She is without proper feeling," he told himself. "She cares nothing for me, of course; but she ought to have some regard for what a man may think of her,

and she seems quite callous to that consideration."

Gay was too much preoccupied at the
moment to think of anything but Pelter's
business. He had brought her a note
containing a peremptory summons. Her
father must see her at once ; she was to
come the next day. This was embarrass-
ing, for she was very much engaged next
day. She never went out in the morning,
having Jim's lessons and the housekeeping
to attend to ; some people were coming
to luncheon, and she would have to help
in entertaining them—it would be impossible to steal off for a solitary walk ;
and she and Sophy had to spend the
evening at the vicarage, where there was
a mild festivity, consisting of tea and
cake, a lecture by a lady on the Zenana
Mission, and a collection.

There was only one way in which she could comply with her father's wish. She would excuse herself on the plea of indisposition from accompanying Sophy—no other excuse would be accepted; and go to Kelvers after dark. It was dangerous, and she hated the sense of petty manœuvring; but she must run the risk of being met and recognized, or of her absence being discovered, and she must bear the degradation of scheming and acting in an underhand fashion.

It was with a heavy heart that she made ready for that evening's gaiety. Sophy too prepared for it in a dejected frame of mind, so cast down by her certainty that Mrs. Fletcher would have the social distinction she had anticipated for herself, that she could not take pleasure in her attire of heliotrope satin, nor in the

pale pink frock which went so well with
Gay's complexion and hair. What good
did it do her to feel sure that no two
women at the castle would be more be-
comingly attired, when Gay's triumph
was given to another ?

Her gloomy previsions were realized.
The young ladies were much more
numerous than the dancing men, and the
precious attentions of the latter naturally
fell to girls who were better worth them
than Miss Rushton. Gay was not worse
off than a good many of her fellow-guests ;
but only a few invitations to dance fell
to her lot, and she made no special impression. Mabel received a great deal
more attention ; and Sophy hung her head
before Mrs. Fletcher's complacent smile,
and felt provoked at the apathy Gay
displayed. She looked on with an absent,

fixed smile on her lips, as if she were there merely as a spectator, and did not care to take a part.

" It is vexatious that you aren't dancing," said Sophy.

" I don't mind—I don't care to dance," said Gay, bringing her thoughts from the gloomy road to Kelvers back to the brightly illuminated room.

" I told James to find you partners, but he has done next to nothing."

" Never mind; I am quite content to look on."

" That isn't what I brought you for," fretted Sophy. " I wish you wouldn't look so absent, Gay—that isn't the way to make men want to dance with you. You ought to pay attention to what is going on."

" Yes, dear," said Gay, meekly, " I will.

I was thinking of something else. Mabel looks very nice, doesn't she ?" seizing on the first remark that occurred to her to change the subject.

It was not a speech to please Mrs. Mildmay. She coldly regarded Mabel, who was gliding past in a waltz with Thornburgh.

"Yes, she looks very well," she said. " It is very strange that Miles hasn't asked you to dance"—in a tone of acute irritation.

"We were rather late, you know. I suppose he had engaged himself for everything before we came."

"But that is no reason. He might have kept some dances for you. I do think," said Mrs. Mildmay, solemnly, and paused — "I do think," she resumed, "that after he was so long at our house, the least he could do would be to dance two or three times with you. I hate changeable people."

Fortunately Mrs. Mildmay's other neighbour, Mrs. Saville, addressed her at that moment, and she was diverted from the contemplation of Thornburgh's neglect. That neglect was no cause of grief to Gay. She was smarting still with the remembrance of his words and manner when they met in the dusk; she had felt later all they could express, and she shrank from receiving perfunctory attentions from him and listening to constrained attempts to talk nothings.

She had been roused from her abstraction by Sophy's grumbling, and her eyes followed the couple who had ruffled her stepmother's equanimity. As she watched them, a passionate revolt against circumstance stirred within her. Others were gay and light-hearted, and she sat among them with her dark secret; others were respected and tenderly guarded, and she was scorned and had to carry a burden of wrong alone and unhelped. The man who was smiling down at Mabel now with that gentle protecting expression might have been *her* lover; and he had looked at her with utter disgust and would always think of her as a liar. It was more than she could bear.

Mabel presently passed on Thornburgh's arm, and stopped for a moment.

"Oh, Gay, I wish that you had been dancing," she said; "it was such a delicious waltz."

"There is quite a scarcity of dancing men," observed Mrs. Saville, good-naturedly.

"It always is so at country balls," said

Sophy, with an air of profound contempt for country festivities.

"Can you give me the next and fourteen, Miss Rushton?" asked Thornburgh.

Gay bit her lip and reddened slightly at the invitation.

"With pleasure," she said quietly, after a brief pause.

The next was a waltz. When it began, Thornburgh came for her with a strange mingling of reluctance and eagerness. He did not want to dance with her—he had been too much chafed that afternoon to be in the mood to make civil pretences. And yet, ever since she had come he had been casting furtive glances at her, and as he looked she drew him.. He had never found her more charming in looks than she was that evening, irritating as it was that his eyes would dwell on her with pleasure.

She danced well, keeping perfect time, and moving lightly and smoothly; but, after a turn or two, she signified that she wished to stop.

"That will do," she said. "I will go back to Sophy now."

"Already? Are you tired so soon?"

"I am not tired," she replied composedly; "but I don't wish to inflict myself on you unmercifully. That would be a poor proof of my gratitude for the invitation which you were obliged to give me. I am really sorry that you thought it necessary to sacrifice yourself."

She spoke in a clear level tone, and looked straight before her, holding her head high.

"Surely you don't imagine that I should

not have asked you to dance in any case?"

"Oh, you have made gallant efforts to show nobody but myself that you disapprove of me. You are very kind. But you have made your offering to politeness, and we needn't do any longer just now what gives neither of us any pleasure."

"But you are quite wrong. It gives me a great deal of pleasure to dance with you. You are the best partner I have had to-night. Pray give me another turn."

"I do not understand how it can give you pleasure to have anything to do with me when you think badly of me," she said coldly.

"But one may change one's way of thinking."

She looked at him with a gleam of incredulous hope in her eyes. Had he faith enough in her, after all, to trust her against appearances ?

" To-night I feel that I was priggishly severe," he said, with a glance of more open admiration than she had ever received from him before. " I am a convert to your view, that a misstatement is not a serious matter, and one ought to make excuses for it from a lady."

" I would rather you despised me for ever than that you excused me in *that* way," she said, in a low vehement tone. " Take me back to Sophy, please."

She put her hand on his arm, and moved on with a decision that was not to be gainsaid. He could only obey her, and then he retired to a corner where he fell a prey to Mr. Saville, who was rejoiced to find an auditor who listened passively, without attempting more than monosyllabic answers. It spoils conversation sadly when one's interlocutor insists on having his turn.

Mr. Saville's enjoyment was broken upon at last by Thornburgh's discovery that a waltz was beginning which he had to dance with Mabel. She was not with her mother, and it was only after a little search that he found her sitting in a quiet nook with Mr. Ashton.

"This is our dance, I think," said Thornburgh.

"Oh, Miles, would you mind letting me off? I am tired now, and I promised to sit this out with Mr. Ashton. You don't mind?"

"How do you expect me to answer that question?" he rejoined, smiling.

Mabel did not smile in return; she looked uneasy and apologetic.

"I should like to rest a little," she murmured.

"Of course you must rest if you are tired," said Thornburgh, in a carelessly kind tone. "I will let you off with a good grace."

He was going away, and Mabel rose and took a few steps after him.

"You might ask Gay," she said hurriedly. "I wish you would. She hasn't had many partners to-night, and it is such a pity."

Mr. Ashton caught the drift of the quickly spoken aside, and was profoundly touched by the little incident. It showed such kindly thought on Miss Fletcher's part, such consideration for a less fortunate sister, such superiority to ordinary feminine jealousy, and so on. In his admiration, he likened the fair girl to an angel as she stood before her cousin. (Mr. Ashton was sure to hit upon a well-worn formula for his thoughts; his wit was very fond of the roadway.)

But Thornburgh looked at Mr. Ashton's angel with anything but approval in his contracted brows. He was angry, most unreasonably angry that his little cousin should recommend Gay to his attention. It roused a curious jealousy in him that anybody should interfere between them, and he resented it on Gay's account; it was like a schoolgirl patronizing a princess.

" Thanks, Mabel, you are very thoughtful," he said drily. "No doubt Miss Rushton would be grateful to you, if she knew. But, unluckily, I am out of her good graces at present."

He withdrew, and Mabel sat down with a somewhat dismayed expression.

" Miles seems quite vexed. I only asked him to dance with Miss Rushton. Do you think there was any harm in that ? " she appealed to her companion, who enthusiastically assured her that her action must be rated high even among the noble deeds of a most unselfish nature.

" She hasn't been dancing much ; she doesn't know many people, you see, and I was sorry to see her sitting down so often. It must be so dull for her. I don't see why my cousin should dislike my speaking about it."

Mabel was something like her aunt Sophy in her gift for threshing out a subject, and she wondered and justified herself a little longer. Mr. Ashton reassured her to the best of his ability, suggesting that Thornburgh's ungraciousness had been caused by disappointment at losing the dance, and presently Mabel smiled with recovered complacency.

" I might have refrained from snubbing Mabel, poor little girl; she meant well," reflected Thornburgh. " But certainly she was ill-inspired in her kindness. Ask Gay! I wish I could—I wish I dared. But I dare not; that is the mournful truth. She would be angrier than she is already. She will not give me the dance she has promised, much less grant me any more. What is to be done with a proud impracticable creature who won't make a truce on any terms, and fires up at a suggestion that one will give her the benefit of her sex, and overlook a little lack of veracity ? "

What, indeed ! One thing was clear,

that he could not persist in his judgment of her; the spirit that preferred the full responsibility and blame of wrong-doing to the easy forgiveness which only meant contempt had something noble in it which wrung esteem from him.

A vision of her pale scorn of his admiration came before him, and made Mabel's serene prettiness seem very tame and commonplace; and as he mentally set the two faces side by side, he was fain to confess that his expedient for casting Gay out of his mind was a failure.

He had done his best to train his heart in the way it should go; he had paid diligent attention to Mabel, and steadily contemplated all her gifts and graces; but with all his efforts he had never been able to "reason himself into a rapture." Mabel was prettier than Gay, unquestionably;

she was trustworthy and truthful, and Gay
was neither one nor the other; she had
been brought up much more carefully.
All this was quite true; but all this was
nothing to the point. With all her dis-
advantages, Gay was the one that could
make him feel; it used to thrill him with
pleasure to meet her glance, or to feel her
sleeve brush his as she walked beside
him; but he could look at Mabel as calmly
as he looked at her mother, and the touch
of her hand had no magic in it. He did
not long for a private talk with her, or
care to scheme to meet her. He had
found her society soothing lately, but the
very qualities which had been pleasant to
his irritated mood would prove insipid and
wearying in time. Gay had stirred him
up, stimulated him, and made him feel
more alive.

No, it wouldn't do, he told himself impatiently; he had made a gross blunder when he imagined it possible to be satisfied with what his cousin could give him. He cared more for one look from Gay than he did for a day of Mabel's sweetest smiles. That passionate, " I would rather you despised me for ever," rang in his ears, and moved him as no words of Mabel's had ever done. Fortunately he had not committed himself during his fit of blindness; he had never made love to Mabel, and so given her a claim on his honour. He was free to withdraw.

For the rest of the evening he danced and talked as was required of him, doing his duty in a mechanical fashion. He presented himself as an unavoidable form for his second dance with Gay, expecting to be told that she was tired. But she rose and took his arm at once, smiling and speaking quite amiably. She did not intend to be openly on bad terms with him—no doubt she wished to hide the state of things from the Mildmays.

He was almost sorry to find her so approachable—he preferred her mood of defiant indignation. But he philosophically reflected that it was well to enjoy what pleasure he could obtain, and it was undeniably pleasant to dance with her, to look at her, to see her smile. The consciousness of their estrangement gave a peculiar zest to the momentary show of friendliness.

When Mrs. Fletcher and her daughter were going home, the former said—

"How was it that you only danced three times with Miles, Mabel? I thought you promised him another waltz."

"I was tired, mother, and I wanted to talk to Mr. Ashton, so I asked Miles to excuse me."

"You wanted to talk to Mr. Ashton! But, my dear, I am afraid poor Miles wouldn't like that—he would be disappointed. And when you are at a ball, you might as well get as much dancing as you can; you can talk to Mr. Ashton at other times. Your cousin's conversation is much more interesting."

"I don't think so," said Mabel, calmly.

"My dear Mabel!"

"Well, mother, I don't. Miles is too clever for me, I suppose—I don't care for the things he cares for. I told you so before. Mr. Ashton talks in a far pleasanter way."

"Why, Mabel, you and Miles have seemed to get on so well."

"Oh, I like him, of course"—in a tone of placid indifference.

"And he likes you, too."

"Not in the way you mean, mother. I know what you have been thinking, but I am sure he doesn't really care for me, except as a cousin. It would be a great pity if he did; for I shouldn't like to marry him."

The dance and the attention she had received had excited Mabel to the point of speaking so freely. It was rather startling to her mother that the docile daughter was taking an independent view of the situation; and it was a blow to find that things were not to run smoothly to the end she desired. But if Mabel was not disposed towards her cousin, nothing could be done. Mrs. Fletcher would never attempt to influence her daughter against her own feelings.

CHAPTER IX.

A NEW SUGGESTION.

"Es ist so elend, in der Fremde schweifen."
Faust.

A LITTLE after half-past seven on the evening of the morrow, Gay descended from her room, dressed for walking. There was little danger of being met. Sophy had gone to the vicarage, Jim was in bed, and Mr. Mildmay was at dinner with Thornburgh, whom he had asked to relieve his solitude. Still Gay went softly, and cast cautious glances round as she came down the stairs, to assure herself that the way was clear.

She reached the schoolroom unobserved, and let herself out by a window which opened to the ground.

It was a stormy evening. The wind blew freshly, chasing great clouds before it, and every now and then a heavy shower of rain fell. It was a long dreary walk in the dark, along the muddy roads; and Gay, who was fatigued already by the late hours of the day before, was very tired when she reached Kelvers.

But her father did not notice her worn-out expression and languid step, nor did he utter any regrets that she should have had to come so far at such a time. He received her with grumbles. She was awfully late. Could she not have contrived to come before?

She explained how she had been engaged all the afternoon.

"Surely you might have come in the morning, then?"

"It would not have been easy. I have to look after the housekeeping and teach Jim; and it would seem strange if I went out for a long walk before luncheon."

Mr. Rushton expressed indignation that his daughter should be such a slave in the Mildmay household.

"You might have a holiday after a ball; they surely could not grudge you that."

"They do not grudge me anything, but I don't like to come here at unusual times. Besides, you told me that I had better keep away in the morning, as that woman is here then."

Some weeks before Pelter had been sent away for a few days on a business errand, and it had been necessary to hire a woman in his absence, who since then had come every morning to do the house-work.

"Yes, as a general thing, of course it is better that you should not come in the morning; but for once you might have made an exception. I wrote that I particularly wished to see you. I want to talk over my plans with you."

He spoke with animation, and Gay noticed that he had a look of purpose, instead of the expression of dreamy lassitude which he had worn lately. Was he thinking of going away? Her heart gave a great bound at the hope that her trial was coming to an end. Things could never be as they had been before. Her father's departure would not restore the prospect of happiness which his coming had taken from her. Thornburgh had given her up, and would never trust her again. That grief was not to be cured. But it would be much to have peace of mind, to have no secret comings and goings, not to tremble daily for Sophy's happiness.

Mr. Rushton settled himself comfortably in his chair and went on—

"I never told you, Gay, about the business that made me leave America."

Gay remembered that he had told her he came to England to find her and Sophy, but she prudently refrained from saying so.

"I had something to do with a company which seemed at first very promising, and I invested rather largely in it. But things went wrong; there was deuced bad management"—in a tone of strong feeling. "You wouldn't understand the details, so it's no use going into them. It

seemed that the whole affair was going to
smash, and as I was one of the directors,
it looked very blue for me, and I saw that
it was time to look out for myself. So I
came over the Atlantic to lie low for a
while."

"Should you have lost money, if you
had stayed?" asked Gay.

"Rather! I was afraid at one time that
I might lose every cent I possessed."

"But you saved it by coming away?"

"I saved some; all that I had in the
company seemed hopelessly gone, but I
brought enough to keep me going. I
didn't see why I should lose any more, so
I turned what I could into ready cash."

Gay was ignorant of business details,
but not so dense that she did not clearly
perceive what her father had done. He
had absconded that he might defraud his

creditors. She knew by this time what he was ; but familiarity with his moral defects could not lessen the pain which they gave her, and she shrank with fresh shame at each proof of his degradation.

" I had to keep quiet, and I found that London was not quite retired enough, so I came here. I meant, of course, to look up you and Sophy, as I told you. I had two birds to kill with one stone."

Mr. Rushton added this *coda* to his explanation, bethinking himself of former utterances of his on the subject, and of the necessity of preserving an appearance of consistency.

It was quite true that he had wanted to find his wife and child. He had manliness enough, when he thought of their existence, to wish to support them ; and he had always cherished a general intention to perform that duty when he had made money enough. But he had been much engrossed with the gambling specu- lations by which he lived, and had taken no steps to carry out his intention, till he found himself obliged to endure an interval of repose from business. That was a con- venient season for squaring his accounts with his family. The yearnings of domestic affection were perhaps stimulated by the necessity of relieving the dulness of en- forced inaction, and a desire to display himself in the new character of a prosperous man.

"I thought London was the best place to hide in," said Gay.

"Not always. It was getting a little too warm for me. This place was capital for my purpose. It is out of the way enough for a hermit; and I told Pelter to set a story about that I was in low water and a little touched in the head, which gave people so much to say of me that they would never think of finding out anything more. It was rather neat, that little stratagem, I flatter myself. I did not attempt to conceal myself. Everything was aboveboard, and Pelter talked quite frankly about me. So I have stayed on here, though Heaven knows it is not a desirable residence; and you, poor little girl, have, I am afraid, been more than once tempted to wish me gone."

He looked at her with a smile.

"Oh yes, you must have felt that," he said, with an air of gracious consideration, as she was opening her lips. "I don't blame you. It has been an awkward position for you, between the Mildmays and me. But it will soon be at an end.

The company is looking up, I hear, and promises to pay ; so the danger and fuss will blow over, and I can go back to America before long."

"You will be glad to get back," said Gay, speaking very quietly in the effort to control herself.

"H'm, I don't know about being glad," said Mr. Rushton, suddenly assuming a melancholy air. "Of course, for some things I prefer America to England. I feel that there is no place for me in my own country. But at my age a man begins to get tired of wandering, and would like peace and quiet. I have been thinking that you had better go back with me, Gay, and then I can settle in a place of my own."

"Go back with you!" echoed Gay, scarcely believing her own ears.

"Yes, that will be the best thing for both of us. You would see more, and have a much livelier life than you can have in this God-forsaken place, and you would make a comfortable home for me. It would be more agreeable for you to be dependent on your father than on a stranger like Mildmay. I do *not* like"— with dignity—"to have my only child a sort of upper servant in a stranger's house."

"But, father, it is impossible! How could I leave Sophy without telling her where I was going?"

"Easily enough. What difficulty is there in departing quietly?"

"But I could never see Sophy again, never write to her," cried Gay.

"Well, I dare say Sophy would be perfectly happy without you. And I

have more claim on you than Sophy has.
What is she to you?"

"I—I had no idea that you were
thinking of such a thing. I am afraid it
would hardly answer. You would find
me in your way. You have been accustomed to be quite free."

"Yes, but I am beginning to feel rather
past that sort of thing; and, as I told you,
the chimney corner is assuming attractions
for me. Surely, Gay, you would rather
be with your father than with strangers?"
—in a tone of surprise. "You look quite
amazed."

"It is so sudden," said poor Gay; "and
it would be such a great change."

"Well, of course, the idea is a new
one to you. I have been thinking for
some time that I had better take you with
me. I should like a little home comfort

now.   My health is not what it was.   To
tell you the truth, I am getting uneasy
about it.   I fear that the complaint I have
may prove serious.   Illnesses in such
cases are long and lingering, and I shall
need some one to look after me."

"But"—with a startled look—"you are
not really ill?"

Mr. Rushton shook his head.

"Yes, indeed, I am.   I have been
watching my own symptoms carefully, and
I don't like them at all.   I think that there
can only be one end to them; and I
should not like to be left to the care of
hirelings and to die among strangers."

Gay did not reply at once, but rose and
walked up and down the room.   It was
useless to struggle or protest.   She was
utterly helpless against this plea; she
must do what he asked, and make this

supreme sacrifice. All her chances of peace and content were snatched away by forces too strong for her; and in the first realization of what her father proposed, she chafed desperately against her fate.

Oh, it was cruel that she must give up everything, that not one poor little shred of what she desired could be hers! She must go away secretly, without taking farewell of those she cared for; she must appear ungrateful, deceitful, regardless of their feelings. They would probably think that she had fled with a lover whom she was ashamed to acknowledge before them. "Oh, I cannot—I cannot!" she cried in her heart, as these things rose before her. But yet she must. Necessity was laid upon her.

The sacrifice was not lightened by any tenderness for her father's state; for she did not credit his story. He was not in good health; but the assertion that he was threatened by mortal disease was made, she thought, merely to work on her feelings, and cause her to yield to his wishes. He chose to take her with him, and he hit upon the one plea to which she could not turn a deaf ear. And she must let herself be worked on. She could not tell him that she did not believe him. For Sophy's sake at least she must submit.

Presently she returned to her chair by the fire.

"Oh, father, father!" she cried.

It was a cry of dismay, an involuntary, piteous remonstrance against this last stroke.

But Mr. Rushton heard in it nothing of the kind. To him it was simply an expression of the surprise and grief

which an affectionate daughter would feel
when told that her father was seriously
ill. He enjoyed a luxurious sense of
merit as he contemplated the home life
he meant to lead. He would become an
irreproachable domestic character, and
atone handsomely for any deficiencies in
that department of duty. Gay's exclamation touched him, and intensified his
realization of himself as a tender father.

" My poor child !" he said, in a voice
touched with manly emotion. " You must
not be too much alarmed," he added,
more cheerfully. " It may be some time
before I begin to give you any trouble in
the way of sick-nursing. A comfortable
home and a regular life may keep the
mischief quiet. Perhaps I shall see you
married before I take to my bed."

" Oh no !" she said, shuddering.

" You will not leave me ?—good little girl ! " Mr. Rushton smiled with supreme self - complacency. It really was very pleasant to be a fond parent.

" You are very like your mother, Gay— wonderfully like ; you have all her sweetness and affection."

Gay felt a pang of passionate pity for the dead mother, whose sweetness and affection had been so wasted.

" But," he went on, " I must not be selfish, and if a good chance came in your way, you must not lose it for me. With your looks you ought to do very well. I shall be proud of my handsome daughter."

She wondered bitterly whether her looks could be turned to profitable account in his business transactions. Perhaps he meant to use her as a means of attracting people to his house. Her heart sank within her as her imagination suggested the possibilities and dangers of the life that lay before her. She was not ignorant—she could very well picture it. The ups and downs, the ignoble schemes, the doubtful society, she saw it all, and she hated it with all her strength.

"I do not want admirers," she said coldly.

"Oh, you will want them when they turn up — you aren't so destitute of feminine weakness. You will relish the attention that a pretty girl with money commands. It will be pleasanter than teaching Mildmay's brat, and hearing the old ladies here prose. You must go? Well, you must not be too late."

He bade her good night in an unusually affectionate manner, and she hurried away. She could bear no more just then. It was too much to be assured that when she flung herself into the sea of troubles before her she would find it an enjoyable place.

Pelter appeared from the back regions, and opening the door for her, followed her out.

" It's late for a lady to be out alone, miss," he said. " I'd better go with you."

" Thank you—you are very kind," she said.

The little attention touched her ; she felt in anticipation the forlornness of the future, and any token of good will seemed precious.

Pelter followed her, rejoiced that he could do her any service. He pitied her as a sufferer from her father, and he cherished a profound liking for her because of the gentle courtesy with which she always treated him. He had been silent about his meeting her in town simply to give her a better chance of escape. Mr. Rushton would be more determined to find her, if he knew she had fled from him. The surly tone which had angered Thornburgh the day before was only an expression of Pelter's disgust at his employer's unreasonable demands. He was as civil to her as he knew how to be, but he always felt too rough and awkward to behave with the respect he would have liked to show.

As he went now, he occupied himself in free mental expression of his opinion about her father. "What has he been saying to make her look like that? He won't be satisfied till he has worried her life out. Oh, Lord, what *are* such people allowed to live for? They only plague and pester everybody that belongs to them. Anybody but *him* would be ashamed to see her at all—the least he could do would be to keep dead and out of the way."

Presently Gay spoke to him, putting a question about her father's health. Had Pelter noticed a change for the worse since they had been at Kelvers?

" No, miss, I think he's much about the same as I've known him before. He gets low with being so quiet, but he'd be all right if he was doing something."

" You would like to go away, no doubt? You must prefer living in your own country."

" England is my country, miss, but I've

lived a good deal out of it. I've knocked about in different places."

" You wouldn't like a settled life, perhaps ? "

" I don't know, miss; I take it as it comes. Some folks can't have likings."

" That is very true," said Gay, with a sigh.

" I've always been one of that sort," went on Pelter, after a pause. " Other men I've known have got on, but I never did. Once I had a piece of luck, a real good chance; but good luck is of no use to folks like me. It slips through their fingers, and I lost mine of course."

" What a pity ! How was it ? " asked Gay.

She was always sorry for the unfortunate ; she could enter into the tragedy of defeat, and something in the sullen bitterness of the man's tone answered to her mood then.   She knew how it felt to have the great chance of one's life snatched from one by ruthless circumstance.

Pelter hesitated, doubtful of the reality of her interest, but he went on—

"It was this way, miss.   I was out in the States, and I had a share in a mine. It didn't do well for some time, and I got sick of the whole concern and went away from the place, and tried my luck at something else.   Then I fell ill and I got into very low water.   One day I was talking to a man I knew, and I said I'd sell my chance of getting anything out of that mine for an old song, and he said he would trade if I liked.   I told him squarely how it was, but he was willing to try it.

Well, a bit after, I found that when I sold, my partners had just found silver."

"What a pity that you didn't know in time!"

"I ought to have known, miss. They had sent me a wire about it, but there was some mistake in the name, and the man that bought my share got it, and kept it from me. Oh, he knew very well what he was doing when he got me to sell!"

"What a shameful cheat!" exclaimed Gay.

"Yes, miss, he was, I think."

"Did he make much by it?"

"Yes; he got a pretty good pile."

"And you couldn't get anything from him?"

"No; not then. But I mean to have it out of him some day!" said Pelter, in a tone which made Gay start; so deep was the grudge it expressed.   Then he added, in his usual manner, " You'll soon be at home, miss.   I'd better go no further."

" Ay, it was a shame !" he said to himself as he plodded back.   " She didn't guess that it was her father that did me in that way.   No, I'm sure she didn't. I should be sorry for her to know ; and he must be kept in the dark till the right time comes !"

CHAPTER X.

AN ACCIDENTAL ENCOUNTER.

"I know the way she went."

Maud.

MR. MILDMAY and his guest had just finished sitting over their wine after dinner, when it was announced to the former that one of his tenants had called to see him. He grumbled at the man's coming at that unseasonable hour, but rose to go to the study, where he saw such people.

"I am sorry to leave you, Miles," he remarked; "you must entertain yourself till I come back."

"I should like to write a letter or two while you are busy," said Thornburgh. "There are some that I mean to write when I get home, and I may as well do them now, if you will allow me."

"Certainly, certainly. You had better go to the schoolroom; you can write comfortably there."

Mr. Mildmay led him thither, and provided him with writing materials. Thornburgh wrote a letter, and then fell into a brooding reverie. There were no special traces of Gay's occupation of the room to remind him of her—neither book nor work was lying about; but it seemed as if something of her lingered there, and brought her more vividly before his mind than any other room in the house.

For the hundredth time he went over his memories of their intercourse; he

recalled the various phases in which she
had presented herself since she had come
—embittered, brusque, and defiant—to beg
help for Sophy, and wondered how much
of her real self there had been in any
aspect which he had seen. These thoughts
were engrossing, and time passed quickly
as he indulged them.

Presently a slight noise roused him from
his abstraction. It sounded as if some
one was cautiously opening the window.
He listened, and heard the window softly
closed, then the bolt was fastened.

"It can't be a burglar; even a burglar
in his dotage would not cut off his own
retreat!" reflected Thornburgh. "One of
the servants has broken bounds. I wish
I had time to disappear—— Ah!"

The curtains had parted, and Gay was
standing staring at him with white cheeks.

Her cloak was wet and marked with mud; a coil of her hair had fallen over her shoulder, and raindrops lay bright upon it.

For a moment they looked at each other; he feeling little less disconcerted than she did.   Then he spoke.

"Don't stand there," he said almost sharply.   It was unbearable that she should look at him with that helpless, frightened expression.

She had recovered herself and advanced slowly.

"I was startled at first," she said.   "I thought the room would be empty."

"I am sorry I am in your way.   I thought you were at the vicarage."

"No; I did not go.   I am in my own room with a bad headache.   And I went out for a little fresh air.   I felt so restless and feverish that I couldn't sleep!"—in a tone of mocking defiance.

"I see," rejoined Thornburgh, gravely. "You have only taken a turn in the garden, of course?"—glancing at her muddy boots and drenched apparel.

"Oh, of course! It would be impossibly improper to go further so late, wouldn't it?"

She laughed, with a great effort to keep up a flippant manner; but she could not hide her nervous uneasiness.

"Let me take your cloak off; you are wet through. How can you be so reckless?" he said, in a low remonstrant tone.

She looked at him, trying to smile and carry off her escapade with a high hand; but suddenly her face changed. An expression of deadly fear came into it, and she clasped her hands convulsively on his arm.

"I hear somebody coming," she whispered. "You will say nothing—pray, pray——"

She snatched the cloak from him and fled behind the curtains. She had just disappeared when Mr. Mildmay entered.

"Sorry to have left you so long, Miles; but old Wren has only just gone. He is awfully long-winded. Come to the study now and have a cigar. Not finished your letters?"

"I have nearly finished. I will come in two minutes. Don't wait for me; I'll be with you directly."

Mr. Mildmay withdrew; and Gay came out of her hiding-place.

"Thank you," she said. Then hesi-

tatingly, after a pause, " You will not tell
any one about to-night ? "

" Is it likely that I would ? " he answered
resentfully.

" No, no—I know you won't," she
murmured.

" You need not be afraid that I will
betray your secrets.   But why have you
to hide things ? "

" Oh "—in a tone of heartsick impatience—" I cannot help myself—if only
I could !   Good night."

" Gay ! " he exclaimed, seizing her hand
as she passed him.

She drew her ice-cold fingers away with
a quick decided movement, and was gone.

He lingered a few minutes where she
had left him, feeling still the clutch of her
hands on his arm, seeing again the pale,
terror-stricken face raised in entreaty to

him.   There was a smile on his lips and
an excited light in his eyes ; he looked as
though he had learnt some very good
news.

"I will see her to-morrow, and then she
shall tell me the whole thing," he said to
himself.   "She can't take me in any
longer, try as she may ; she has betrayed
too much."

He rose next day with a vague sense
of well-being, which presently resolved
itself into a definite satisfaction, as he
thought of the explanation which he had
determined to have with Gay.   He would
see her as soon as possible.   After the
days in which he had struggled to put her
out of his head, and their intercourse had
been only painful, it was an exquisite relief
to be able to anticipate pleasure in a meeting with her.   The dreariness of the time

of estrangement had taught him how dear she was; but he had learnt it better when he felt the eager bound with which his heart turned to her as she clung to him, and he read in her terror that the secret of her conduct was altogether different from what he had supposed it to be.

The day began gladly; the sun shone more brightly than it had done lately; there was a breath of spring in the air. A cloud had lifted since it had become possible that his belief in Gay might be restored.

After luncheon he went to Westby Lodge. If he could not contrive some private talk with her at the house, he would find out in what direction she intended to walk and join her. He was disappointed. Gay was with Sophy. No opportunity of speaking to her alone offered; and she was not going to walk that afternoon, she was going to drive with her stepmother.

Thornburgh had no better luck the next day, nor the next. He went to Westby Lodge, but she was not visible; he lay in wait for her on the road to Kelvers, but he did not fall in with her.

It was not till Sunday that he saw her again, when she was in her place at church. He felt it fortunate that his seat commanded a good view of that assigned to Mr. Mildmay's family. He could see Gay's profile very well, as he sat behind her; and he spent time which should have been devoted to listening to the sermon in studying her, and thinking how pale and tired she looked. Mr. Ashton was preaching that morning on

the temptation of Abraham, and in point-
ing out the difficulties which the patriarch
must have felt in offering his son as a
sacrifice, he suggested that Abraham must
have shrunk from the criticism of his
household, and wondered what the
servants would say of his act. This touch
of original thought—the very first that
Mr. Ashton had displayed in that pulpit—
did not rouse Thornburgh from the abstraction in which he was vowing that he
would find some way of freeing Gay from
the care that weighed upon her.

" Probably it isn't half so bad a business
—this dreadful mystery—as she imagines,
foolish child, and if she would speak out
it might all be put straight. Anyway, I
can deal with it better than she can, and
she shall not be troubled any longer."

After service, Thornburgh joined the

Mildmay party, and being invited to luncheon, accepted promptly. They were walking, and while Sophy and her husband paused at the churchyard gate to exchange civilities with some of their neighbours, Thornburgh went on with Gay, who hurried off, holding Jim by the hand. He kept resolutely at her side the whole way, and he was helped in this by Sophy, whose pace was not to be quickened that morning by any effort of Mr. Mildmay.

Gay was very silent on the walk, and Jim had a fine opportunity for chatter, which he did not throw away. He was in good spirits; the choir had nearly broken down in chanting the Psalms, and this little incident had greatly enlivened him, and he was looking forward to the afternoon, when a service for children was to be held. He particularly affected these services ; but he had not purchased for himself a good degree by his diligent attendance at them, for it was his repre- hensible practice to try to make the Sunday scholars laugh, and to this end he would make grimaces, or answer *à tort et à travers* in the catechizing. To-day he gleefully anticipated a special treat, and he generously pressed Gay to share his pleasure. He had learnt that three babies were to be christened that afternoon, and this he declared was an opportunity that ought not to be lost, for among three there was sure to be one that would cry, and it was great fun to hear crying in church.

"I don't like to hear a baby cry," said Gay, smiling, "but I will go with you, if you wish it, Jim."

This arrangement would leave Thornburgh no chance of speaking to her alone, and he chafed as he listened. But he must make an opportunity, if none was given him, and he resolved to go to church too, and dispose of Jim's intrusive presence in some fashion.

At luncheon, Mr. Mildmay was full of a great piece of news which had been communicated to him after church by the village constable. A burglary had taken place at a house in the neighbourhood, and a large sum of money and some valuable diamonds had been carried off.

"Jackson told me that he believes it has been done by those men at Kelvers; he feels quite sure that there is something wrong about them, and he means to watch them. He warned me to be careful about this house—says he has noticed one of the men hanging about the grounds in the dusk. I shall have Rollo turned loose at night."

Rollo was a big fierce mastiff, who would certainly not suffer any stranger to enter the house.

"How very unpleasant to have such people in the neighbourhood," said Sophy. "Isn't it true that a maniac is living at Kelvers?"

"Jackson thinks that is only talk, and they are really shady characters."

"I hope they won't come here," remarked Mrs. Mildmay.

"I shall take my catapult to bed every night," cried Jim. "I should like to see a burglar; it would be fun, Gay, wouldn't it?"

Gay had listened to Mr. Mildmay's remarks with unmoved visage, but her very composure showed that she was not undisturbed. If she had been indifferent she would naturally have expressed some interest and curiosity about his news.

She looked up with a faint smile at Jim's address, and met Thornburgh's gaze fixed upon her. She winced, and turned away quickly, changing colour. Mr. Mildmay began to speak, and she could not answer Jim. She drew a long breath, and looked straight at Thornburgh across the table, sending a mute defiance to him.

"Why do you watch me? You shall not find out anything—I am *not* afraid," her expression said as plainly as words could have done.

His pulse quickened a little as he saw the pale set face and the resolute eyes. They were coming to close quarters; this was better than the glacial distance at

which they had been lately. He accepted
her challenge—she should not keep her
secret much longer.

After luncheon he went into the garden,
and waited till Gay and Jim should
appear. Jim presently came out with one
of the housemaids.

"Gay isn't going," he told his cousin.
"She says she has a headache, so Sarah
is taking me."

Thornburgh returned to the house and
took leave; then he went by the short
cut to Thornburgh Hall, passed through
the grounds, and struck into a field path
which brought him out on the moorland
road to Kelvers. He did not go on
towards the house, but turned and walked
slowly in the opposite direction. It was
not long before he saw the person he was
looking for.

CHAPTER XI.

ON THE MOOR.

" Our souls in us were stirred and shifted
　　By doubts and dreams and foiled desires.

*　　　　*　　　　*　　　　*

And one with me I could not dream you;
And one with you I could not be."

SWINBURNE.

GAY came towards him, walking at a rapid pace, and he hastened his steps. When she recognized him, she paused for a moment, but immediately recovered herself, and advanced as quickly as before. She put back her veil as she came near, and looked at him with eyes full of dark fire.

"You are watching me, Mr. Thornburgh," she said in a biting tone.

"I am watching for you," he rejoined. "I have been trying for some days to get an opportunity of speaking to you, as you know, but you have kept so carefully out of my way that I am obliged to meet you as I can."

"If you know that I have kept out of your way, you know that I do not wish to see you, and you might have respected my wishes, I think. You have nothing to say to me that I desire to hear."

"Still I must persist in requesting you to hear me," he said quietly. "I have to acknowledge a blunder and to apologize for an injustice—you cannot be ungenerous enough to refuse me an opportunity of relieving my conscience."

"I am not generous at all, Mr. Thornburgh, I assure you—you double your blunder if you imagine it; and I don't care to listen to your acknowledgments or your apologies."

"You are angry with me."

"Yes, I am. I am too angry to give you a hearing." She stopped short and regarded him defiantly. "Can you not leave me alone?" she cried impetuously. "Why will you thrust yourself into my affairs? The only thing I want from you is to let me go my way in peace."

"I will do as you ask in five minutes," he returned, unmoved.

Her opposition had only strengthened his determination; he divined that she wanted to rouse his wrath by her open hostility, and drive him away, and he was not to be beaten in that fashion.

"Give me five minutes—that is a small

favour—and then, if you order it, I will go," he persisted.

She did not answer in words, but she walked on, summoning her courage and pride to her aid. She would want all she possessed in the coming interview, she felt sure; the change in his manner since Thursday had filled her with dread. She saw that he was sorry for her—perhaps he wanted to help her, and her heart quailed at the prospect of resisting him. It would be easier to bear coldness and bitter speeches than to refuse his kindness and deny him her confidence.

"In the first place, I have to confess that I have discovered myself to be very dense," he began. "You have taken me in completely by the comedy you have played. You had grave reasons for hiding your visits to Kelvers, and when they

were discovered you threw dust in my
eyes by pretending that you went for a
mere caprice, and resorted to deception
out of levity. It was clever of you to hit
upon that way of defending the secret;
but it is useless to attempt to impose upon
me any longer—you can't make me believe
that you are the frivolous deceiver you
chose to paint yourself. I shall always
be ashamed of your success. I ought to
have known you better."

"Are you sure? You know very little
of me," she said drily.

"Forgive me for my stupidity, and let
us be friends again."

"That would be difficult," she returned
quickly. "You have distrusted me once.
You would never trust me thoroughly
again, and one ought to believe in one's
friends. Besides, you forget. You had

good reason for what you thought. You knew that I was acting in an underhand deceitful way. You were not stupid at all."

" I was very stupid in not knowing that you must have had a strong and good motive for acting as you did. When I look back, I feel so ashamed of my mistake that I scarcely dare hope you will pardon it. I wronged you grievously."

"Oh, your opinion was not a matter of great importance," she said in a hard light tone. ("If I could only offend him," she was thinking desperately, "he would go away.") " But I object to your new idea that I had a serious reason for concealment. I think it would be more polite on your part to believe my own account. What great secret could I have? You don't believe, I suppose, that Kelvers is inhabited by burglars, and that I am in their counsels ?"

She laughed. He used to hate that flippant, forced laugh; now it sounded only mournful in his ears.

"I do not believe that, of course," he answered quietly. "I suppose that for some reason or other you feel bound to show kindness to this man, that he has good cause for wishing to keep in seclusion, and that you are obliged to conceal your acquaintance with him. He has— or you imagine he has—a claim on you, and you can be absurdly generous and self-forgetful; that is my theory. You would not dread discovery so much as you do, if it might not be dangerous to this person. You would not visit him as you did on Thursday merely to amuse yourself."

As he spoke, she paled and her eyes sank; but, rallying her forces, she looked up steadily at him.

"Oh, you don't know *what* a girl would do who is capable of meeting a man in the dusk, as if she were a housemaid flirting," she said mockingly.

For a moment that taunt shook his composure.

"Ah, forget that odious speech!" he said vehemently. "If you knew how disgusted I was with myself as soon as I had made it! It was too atrocious for you to resent. You must feel sure that I scarcely knew what I was saying. I was too angry and chafed at our coolness to be in my right mind. Forgive me. You *must* forgive that, and never think of it again."

He made a pause, but she did not

speak, and he went on in his former quiet manner.

"You may find your position very difficult. You are young, and you have no one to advise or protect you. Let me help you. Look upon me as your brother, and let me manage for you. I will keep your secret as carefully as you would, and I will do all that can be done for you in this trouble."

"You can do nothing. There is nothing to be done," she said in an expression-less tone—expressionless because it was a great effort to command her voice at all.

"You cannot be sure of that till we have talked the case over. Two heads are better than one."

She was silent.

"Will you not let me help you?"

"You can do nothing," she repeated, in the same dull tone as before.

"Will you not at least let me try?" he said, gently and urgently.

"But I tell you there is nothing to be done. Nothing—nothing!"—with a sudden outburst of irritability. He was torturing her by his offered help, and she was in no condition to bear fresh pain patiently. "You are very good, Mr. Thornburgh, but you are labouring under a delusion when you press your assistance and protection upon me. I don't need either. What can I say to make you understand that it would be better not to interfere in other people's affairs?"

She looked at him, meeting his eyes full, bearing without flinching his half-reproachful, half-entreating gaze.

"Very well; if that is all your answer

I can only leave you alone," he said coldly.

He lifted his hat and walked quickly back. He had failed completely, and his failure mortified him inexpressibly. He had been so eager to make peace with her and to return to their old relations. It was galling to find no answering eagerness on her side, to be shown that his proffer of assistance was importunate, and his solicitude superfluous.

He had not gone far, when he heard his name called in a faint voice, and turning, he saw Gay coming with light swift steps towards him. The cloud lifted from his face, and he was at her side in an instant.

"I could not let you go in that way," she said; "it is too odious to seem so ungrateful. I *am* grateful for your goodness ; I shall always thank you for trusting me. Forgive me for my ungraciousness just now."

She held out her hand and smiled at him wistfully and deprecatingly.

"It is you that have to forgive," he said, holding her hand tight.

"No, no; I have forgotten all that. I shall only remember that you were willing to be my brother, and I shall never forget that."

"It would be a pleasanter acknowledgment if you made use of me as a brother."

"Ah, don't say anything more——" She paused, and went on, "I would tell you if I could—indeed, I would. But the secret isn't mine, and I must keep it; and you could not help me if you knew all about it."

"Keep the secret to yourself; I do not

ask to know it.   But the miserable business is wearing you out.   You look ill ; I
cannot bear to see it.   I *must* do something for you, for I love you, dear ; I love
you.   Let me take care of you and stand
by you, even if I can do nothing more.
Be my wife, and then I can keep you safe
from trouble."

She drew back a step or two, and
looked at him with wide startled eyes.

" You ask me that, though you don't
know how I am mixed up in this business ?"

" I ask you to be my wife, so that I may
take you out of it."

" But you don't know what the secret
may be," she insisted.

" I am content not to know.   It cannot
change my feeling ; I know *you*, and I
love you."

She drew a long breath.

"Oh, you do believe in me, after all," she murmured.

He stooped over her, and their lips met. For a moment he held her close; he could feel the beating of her heart, and was sure that she loved him. And she, with his arms round her, knew what despair was.

"You are my own," he said softly, kissing her again.

"Oh no, oh no!" she sobbed, releasing herself. "You must not love me; I cannot be your wife. I ought not to have let you speak."

"Gay!"

"It is true. I cannot be anything to you."

"Why?"

He looked down at her with a smile, as he put the question. He felt com-

posedly confident that he would prevail
this time, for he knew that her heart was
on his side.

" I cannot tell you."

" But, my darling, be reasonable "—in a
tenderly playful tone, as if she had been
a child.   " You must tell me your reasons,
so that I may know what they are worth.
If you cannot tell me, then I shall suppose
that they are an exaggeration of your
fancy, and I won't be sent away.   There
can be no reason against my loving you,
unless——"

" Unless ? " she echoed.

" Unless you are married already," he
ended the sentence, laughing.   " You will
not tell me that that is the case ? "

" Oh, don't laugh ! " she cried, wincing.
" I am in earnest.   No ; I am not married,
but I am as much divided from you as if I

were. I—I——" She hesitated, faltered;
she could find no words. "I am not free,"
she said faintly, at last.

"Not free?" he repeated.

"No; it is impossible that I should be
your wife."

There was a silence. Thornburgh took
her words in their most obvious meaning,
and supposed that she was engaged to be
married; and disgust and indignation were
strong within him. She had behaved
abominably. Every sweet look and word
she had given him had been a cheat; she
had drawn him on to love her when she
was bound to somebody else. That was his
first judgment. She had fooled him completely; and, in the rush of his wounded
feeling, her betrayal of love for him seemed
only an aggravation of her offence. He
did not want love which was stolen from

another man; what good did that do him?

" Thank you for speaking out," he said, with an effort. "It is a pity that you did not make me understand your position sooner; if I had been aware of it I should not have troubled you with attentions which you were not free to accept. I see that my importunity this afternoon was very ill judged. You must set it down to my ignorance that there is a happy man who has a right to advise you and help you."

He did not look at her as he spoke, and he did not see the puzzled expression with which she heard him, or the flash of comprehension which crossed her face at his last sentence. He was gone; and she stared after his rapidly receding figure, amazed at the construction he had put upon her words. He thought her base enough to play with his love, to let him kiss her, while she was bound to another man ?

She started forward, hot eager words of denial and self-justification on her lips. He must not rate her so low. Then she stopped short. She could not undeceive him ; that would be to invite love-making, to which she must not listen. She did not feel able to meet the determination with which he would try to break down her resistance ; her forces were exhausted.

After all, what did it matter ? she asked herself recklessly. He must think ill of her when she went away—a little more or a little less of contempt would make no difference. And he would forget her more easily if he was angry with her.

She turned towards Kelvers and walked

on mechanically. When she reached the house she went round to the back door.

"Let me sit down in the kitchen," she said wearily. "I want to be quiet for five minutes."

Pelter did not look surprised at the request. He led her into the kitchen and disappeared. He returned with a glass of wine, which he set on the table near her.

"You will not be disturbed, miss. Nobody will come here," he said, and left her.

CHAPTER XII.

THE EXPERIENCE OF BALAAM.

> "Sudden stings
> Of fresh pain made her start up from her place,
> And set to some strange unknown goal her face."
>
> W. MORRIS.

PELTER betook himself to the room in which his employer sat, and began to make up the fire.

"Leave that alone," said Mr. Rushton, querulously; "the room is too hot already. It is suffocating, and you needn't try to roast me in addition. It would be better to open a window; but you never have any sense, Pelter."

"Shall I open a window?"

"Yes, do; it will make the atmosphere more endurable."

The window was opened, and the damp west wind rushed in.

"Ugh, what a draught! Shut the window, for Heaven's sake; this is too much for any one."

Mr. Rushton was never equable in mood, and lately he had been very peevish and ill-humoured. He made no attempt to control his irritability, and Pelter took it all with as little show of impatience as if he were a "thing of wood," or were blessed with the sweetness of a saint.

"Do you want anything?" he asked, when he had closed the window.

"I want a good deal that I cannot get here"—fretfully. "I am sick to death of this place, and the sooner I get out of it the better I shall be pleased. I shall go off with sheer dulness, I do believe. I've a good mind to start to-morrow." Mr. Rushton groaned, and moved his position uneasily. "I had an awful night last night. I have got low living in this way, and my nerves are all worn out. Really, I can't stand any more; I will go directly."

"You'll leave Miss Rushton behind, then?" observed Pelter.

"Of course not. She will go with me, as we have arranged."

"You can't go in such a hurry, then."

"That will make no difference. She can leave at any moment. She can't take any luggage with her. She could go to-morrow well enough, I have no doubt. I *will* do it. Give me some paper, Pelter, and I will write to her that she must join me to-morrow in time to catch the last train."

Pelter did not move.

" Rather short notice," he said.

" What does that matter to you ? "

" Nothing to me, or to you, either. So long as you get what you want, it matters nothing about anybody else," said Pelter, in his usual expressionless voice. " Nobody but you would think of dragging your daughter away with you."

Mr. Rushton stared at him astounded.

" My daughter ought to be with her father when he is ill; she would not wish anything else," he said, with an effort at dignity.

" Ill ! " said Pelter, contemptuously. " The very animals have more spirit than that; they go away by themselves to die, and they give no bother. But you must spoil your daughter's life because you fancy you are ill. Do you really believe that she is willing to go?"

Pelter withdrew, still unmoved in face, but with satisfaction warm in his heart.

"Thank the Lord!" he murmured to himself; "he's heard the truth for once, and I've told it to him. He can't think after this that I'm the fool he took me for. 'A good, devoted fellow; stupid, but would do anything for me!' eh, Mr. Rushton? Don't you flatter yourself; the devoted fellow is playing his own game, and wouldn't put up with you for a week, if he didn't mean to get something out of you."

Mr. Rushton was left in a state of as utter amazement as must have overcome the prophet Balaam when his ass opened her mouth and spoke. It was amazing

that the dull, taciturn man should speak
freely at all; it was trebly amazing that
he should speak in such a strain.

Mr. Rushton had firmly believed that
Pelter was full of grateful devotion for
the benefits he had received from him.
When the man was dangerously ill in
a wild place, he had saved his life
by his medical skill and care, and he had
taken him into his service when he was
penniless.   There was an item on the
other side of the account, but this he did
not put into his reckoning; for he had
no suspicion that Pelter had discovered
the way in which he had been tricked.

Pelter owed him a great deal, and looked
up to him with liking and admiration.
This was a matter of course. Mr. Rushton was the victim of a profound confidence in his own powers of attraction,

and always supposed that those admitted to his acquaintance found him charming. The blow which had been dealt that day to this lifelong belief was the first that it had ever really felt, and he was bewildered by the shock, too bewildered to be angry. Pelter had been insufferably insolent, but he overlooked that in the wonder of the fact that Pelter did not think him admirable, did not feel it a privilege to serve him and bask in the light of his presence.

Mr. Rushton, plunged in perturbed reflections on the truly horrible revelation of human selfishness and imbecility that had been made to him, did not hear the door open, and only became aware of his daughter's presence when she spoke. He turned with a start, and frowned as he regarded her.

He had been thinking of Pelter, but the sight of Gay reminded him of the occasion of Pelter's offence, and caused him to speculate as to what truth there was in the man's remarks. The idea that she was really unwilling to go with him had never entered his head ; he had unhesitatingly assumed that she would wish to do so. He was out of health, and a daughter should nurse her father. Besides, who would not gladly minister to a father with such a gift for winning hearts ? The path of duty in this case must be that of pleasure. Gay would never wish to lose the mournful satisfaction of tending his last days.

It was very disagreeable to have this softly tinted picture blurred and darkened by Pelter's coarse brush. Mr. Rushton's selfishness was not of the savage kind which will make its meal on anything; it had refined tastes, and the food it desired must be delicately flavoured, and served with proper sauces. He did not want to drag with him a reluctant daughter, whose melancholy would reproach him and make him dull. He wanted Gay to feel herself lucky in leaving this out-of-the-way place and going with a rich indulgent father to livelier scenes.

Gay repeated what she had heard at luncheon.

"It will not be safe for me to come to Kelvers often after this," she said.

Mr. Rushton nodded. He was watching her closely, and he did not like her looks. She was very pale, with dark shadows under her eyes. There were traces of tears on her face, and her whole expression was languid and dejected.

"Would it be possible for you to go soon?" she asked.

"Are you in such a hurry?"

"I think the sooner we go the better. It is very dreadful to be always afraid," said Gay, wearily. "I am so tired of it."

"There is nothing to be afraid of. You have always managed to come and go without being seen—— You haven't?" —with a quick change of tone. "Who has seen you? Were you asked about it?"

She briefly replied. Mr. Rushton seemed greatly disturbed by her story, and rebuked her for keeping silence on the subject.

"I did not think it necessary to tell you," she said.

"It was decidedly necessary that you should tell me. You knew I wanted to be quiet till I am quite out of the wood, and if this man talks—— "

" He will not."

" Pray, how do you know that ? "

" He is a gentleman; he would never talk of a thing which a lady wished to be a secret," said Gay.

Her father shot a sharp glance at her.

" You have wonderful confidence in him. How old is he ? "

" About thirty."

" Good looking ? "

" Yes."

" He has been staying at Mildmay's— you have seen a good deal of him ? "

" Yes."

" Has he made love to you, Gay ? " jestingly.

She started as if she had felt a touch

on a raw wound. She tried to utter a light meaningless reply, but her quivering lips would not form the words, and she covered her face with her hands.

Mr. Rushton fidgeted.

"What's the matter? Has the fellow treated you badly? Never mind, Gay; you'll pick up somebody else. Don't cry; it spoils your eyes. He isn't worth that sacrifice."

She hastily dried her eyes, and mastered her emotion, grievously ashamed of her breakdown.

"You are wrong, father," she said with dignity. "Mr. Thornburgh has not treated me ill at all; on the contrary. I was not crying on that account."

"Were you crying at the prospect of leaving the neighbourhood of this man?" asked her father, drily.

Gay did not resent the question; she was too worn out to be sensitive.

"I have told you already that I wish to go away as soon as possible," she answered listlessly. "There is nothing between me and him. How could there be, under the circumstances?"

"Oh, I see! I stand in the way," quickly.

She made no rejoinder; she had no energy to deny and protest and say smooth things, and Mr. Rushton, after waiting in vain for the soothing assurances he had intended to draw out, fell back in his chair with a heavy sigh.

There was a silence. Gay regarded the fire with a weary apathy on her face; she had come to the end of her powers of feeling for the time. Her father looked at her, and saw that she was not thinking of him, and that his presence did not affect her in any way. He did not exist for her at that moment.

It was the first time in his life that he felt he was a cipher with one of his family; he had been accustomed in domestic life to fill the stage and play the leading character. Gay's mother — a spirited woman, whom her daughter resembled— had often quarrelled with him, but she had always given him full attention; Sophy had watched him in trembling fear of his temper, and flattered and soothed him with the reckless want of principle which a home despotism produces in a weak woman. Never before had Mr. Rushton seen himself put aside, and it seemed to him as if his world were being transformed by an ill-natured magician.

"Gay, just get me a glass of wine," he said; "I feel upset."

This was true—a faintness had seized him; but it was also true that he made the request with the expectation that it would rouse Gay to a sense of filial duty. His little indispositions had invariably brought him petting before, and in the chill of his new experiences he craved a little warmth of womanly tending.

Gay rose at once, and brought him the wine from the sideboard.

"I am sorry you don't feel well," she said, as he drank off the contents of the glass. "Will you have another?"

She spoke kindly enough, but mechanically, with none of the tender concern which she should have shown.

"Shall I call Pelter?" as the second glass was refused.

"No, I don't want him; he's an un-grateful scoundrel, and cares nothing for me. Nobody does—I am in the way, and the few people that know of my existence would be glad to hear it was over. I think the best thing I could do would be to put an end to myself—then you would have no more trouble with me."

Gay stood beside him, her head droop-ing, her eyes fixed on the floor, unmoved by his outburst.

"Don't talk in that way," she said gently, taking up the decanter and glass to restore them to their places.

"What else can I feel," went on Mr. Rushton, irritated further by her indif-ference, "when I see myself a poor superfluous wretch — when you would be happier if I were dead, and tell me so?"

No eager protest interrupted him. Gay was only aware of a great fatigue. It would be labour lost to point out the injustice of the charge.

" Yes, the sooner I am out of the way the better—I can't make my exit too quickly "—touching the pocket of his coat where he always kept a revolver. " Then you would be free, and you need not go away with me."

Gay was at the sideboard, and he could see her in a mirror opposite. At this dreadful threat she only shrugged her shoulders slightly, and the languid calm of her face was undisturbed. It was by no means the first time that she had heard her father talk of doing after the high Roman fashion. Suicide is a favourite suggestion with a weak, excitable man, when things are not to his mind.

"I must go back directly," she said, "and I should like to know what you intend to do. Can you go away this week? It is not safe to stay now—if anything were found out——"

"I must go this week," he said sullenly. "I have no choice, as you have let your friend know too much; but I don't exactly know what day I can start."

"Can I go alone then?"

It was settled that she should go the next day by the mail to London, and, to secure as much secrecy as possible, she should start from Alverthwaite, a town two miles on the other side of Kelvers, where she was unknown. Mr. Rushton seemed to have forgotten his recent wish to leave the place, and was curiously indifferent about the projected departure. He declared himself to be too tired to fix the day on which he would join Gay, or the place of their meeting.

"We can arrange all that at the last minute," he said fretfully. "You must come here to-morrow night, and then I'll give you money for the journey and tell you where to go. Pelter will walk over the fell to Alverthwaite with you."

As soon as Gay had gone, Pelter presented himself.

"I don't want anything," said Mr. Rushton, not lifting his eyes from the fire, at which he was moodily staring.

Pelter shut the door and advanced into the room.

"Didn't you hear me? I don't want you."

"I must speak to you for a minute, sir," replied Pelter. "It's something important. I caught that woman listening at this door five minutes ago. I don't know how she slipped into the house without my hearing her, but she did ; and she had her ear at the keyhole."

Mr. Rushton tersely expressed a wish about the woman's fate.

"What did you do ? " he added.

"Took her by the arm and marched her into the kitchen. She's locked up there now. If you didn't say anything you mind her hearing—— "

"We were talking of going away. It would be a nuisance if this woman cackled, and Miss Rushton was interfered with. That would never do. Is there any way of gagging her, do you think ? If she could be kept quiet for a day—that is all that is necessary. Miss Rushton starts to-morrow. Give her some money."

He tossed a pocket-book to the man,

and when he was alone, fell into gloomy brooding. Gay had unconsciously followed up the blow which Pelter had given to his egotism by an even sharper stroke. Pelter had been right in his brutal remarks. His daughter was indifferent to him. She loved a stranger, and she was mourning because duty to her father parted her from this man. A very poor companion and nurse she would make, if all the time she was pining for her lover! Mr. Rushton could have adopted James II.'s cry, "God help me, my own child has forsaken me!" and he felt that his position was indeed pathetic, and pitied himself from the bottom of his heart. He did not pity Gay. He never did pity anybody that had to make a sacrifice on his account, and he was not likely to begin that unwonted exercise with his daughter, who, as a daughter,

was, in his opinion, fulfilling the end of
her existence in being a whole offering
on the altar of his claims.

His sense of injury was not lessened by
any suspicion that the lack of enthusiastic
filial devotion which she had shown was
caused by himself, and that he deserved
no better.   He had no conception of the
shame and repulsion which his life had
produced in Gay; for he regarded the
blameworthy passages in his career simply
as misfortunes.   He had certainly run into
a great deal of debt, but that was because
he had been unlucky.   He had never
wished to defraud anybody, and he would
have gladly paid his creditors double if he
had had the money.   As to the doubtful
transactions in which he had been engaged,
he had generally been dragged in ignorance into them by his associates ; and in

the few exceptions to this rule, he had
been the victim of circumstances, and had
been driven by hard necessity to stretch
a point. It has been shown how he regarded his desertion of wife and child, and
how he claimed Gay's compassion for that
painful trial. His conscience had never
given him . any trouble; the conscience
of a thoroughly selfish man, whose one
rule of conduct is to do what he finds
convenient or agreeable, is a weak and
undeveloped organ.

Pelter returned to his prisoner, who
was sitting by the fire with a scared,
uneasy look on her face. She was
about twenty-five, handsome in a rustic
style, with crisp black hair and ruddy
cheeks.

"Well, what have you been saying?" she said, with an attempt to speak

jauntily.   "What have you told the master?"

"Nothing about you, you may be sure," returned Pelter.   "What's the good of telling a poor maniac like that anything to upset him?   I don't want to have a row with him, and I'd be sorry if he hurt you.   And it don't matter if you did hear him; he's bad this afternoon, and only talks nonsense.   You couldn't make head or tail of it."

"It sounded sensible enough, what I heard."

"Ay, it sounds well enough, but if you knew the real facts, you'd know it was all stuff.   He's full of delusions — takes all manner of ideas into his head.   I'm glad he wasn't at his worst.   You'd be frightened to death if you heard him *then*."

"Well, Mr. Pelter, if it don't matter that I heard him, why did you lock me up here?"

"Why, I had two reasons. First and foremost I was scared out of my wits when I saw you." Susan nodded to her self with a knowing smile, as who should say, "Now you are betraying yourself." "For I thought if he happened to catch you there'd be the very deuce to pay. It's no joke when he gets violent, I can tell you. So I hustled you out of the way, and I locked you up because I was put out with you. I can't deny that I felt provoked to see you."

"Ay, ay; I believe *that!*"

"For," continued Pelter, "it really seemed too bad that you should play such tricks. You're welcome to hear his talk —I don't care about *that;* but I do care if he's made worse, and gives me extra trouble. I've told you so, and I thought you weren't the woman to make bother. But, curiosity, curiosity! You can't get a woman without it." He shook his head with melancholy at this conclusion. "However," he resumed, in a cheerful tone, "as it happens, no harm has been done. He didn't find you. But I hope you'll be careful for the future."

"How long do you think the future's likely to be?"

"Lord, how can I tell? He talks every now and then of going away directly, but he won't have the settling of his going— that depends upon his relations. He may stay here for months. It's a mercy that Miss Rushton can come and see him now and then. It does him good. He was an old friend of her father's, and knew her when she was a child, and it always pleases him to have a talk to her."

"Well," said Susan, rising, "I'd like to go now, Mr. Pelter, if you don't object."

Pelter pressed her to remain. Now she had come, she must have some tea. He would be truly thankful to have a companion at his solitary meal. She accepted the invitation. During the repast he made no further reference to her indiscretion, and when she herself returned to the subject and hinted at what she had overheard, he displayed no interest, asked no questions, and seemed only desirous of talking on any other topic than the threadbare one of his employer's delusions.

The effect of this strategy was that when Susan departed, Pelter knew about all that she had heard, and she was sadly convinced that she had gained no such materials for gossip as she had believed. The surprising discovery which she thought she had made was merely a figment of a madman's fancy.

CHAPTER XIII.

"THE CURTAIN'S CUE TO FALL."

" Have I not hideous death within my view,
   Retaining but a quantity of life
   Which bleeds away, even as a form of wax
   Resolveth from his figure 'gainst the fire?"
                                    King John.

PELTER returned to the sitting-room, which was dusky in the early twilight of the grey day.

"Here is your pocket-book," he said. "I daren't give her money—it would be dangerous. I've managed her——"

He broke off short as a flame leaped up in the fire, and threw a strong illumination on Mr. Rushton. He was crouching in

his chair, one hand grasped the table convulsively, his face was drawn with pain.

"Are you ill? Can I get you anything?"

"No, I don't want anything. You
needn't stay."

Pelter hesitated.

"Go away, I tell you," said Mr. Rushton, sharply.

Pelter obeyed, and the other was left
alone to bear the pain which had seized
him.   He had had attacks of pain before
which he had not found easy to endure,
but they had been slight compared to this
burning, stinging agony.   He hated that
Pelter should witness his suffering—"gloat
over it," as he phrased it in the bitterness
roused by the startling revelation of the
man's   real   sentiments   towards   him.
Pelter could do nothing for him, and he

would be glad in his heart to know that he was so ill—Mr. Rushton felt that it would be utterly humiliating to give him such a gratification.

Presently the violence of the pain spent itself. He was weak and worn, but at least he was at ease, and that seemed a priceless boon. As soon as he could move freely, he rang and ordered something to eat. He made a great effort to speak as usual, and lightly referred to his attack as a passing twinge or two.

Pelter gave an account of the way in which he had dealt with Susan, and asked some questions about the arrangements for the departure, taking it for granted that it was to be on the next day. But Mr. Rushton objected to such haste, and decided that he would start on Tuesday evening; that would be quite early enough. When Pelter spoke of the details that had to be settled, he gave absent answers, and at last exclaimed peevishly—

"Don't bother me about it—do as you please. Confound it all, what *do* I care what you do ? I don't care what happens. Life is a hateful business ; I loathe it. I feel more inclined to make an end of it than to go anywhere."

"Oh no, you won't do that, sir," said Pelter, stolidly. "Folks that really mean to do that sort of thing don't let it out beforehand."

This indifference about the journey which Mr. Rushton had professed himself a little while ago so eager to undertake struck Pelter as being what, in American phrase, he bluntly styled "pure cussedness." He was revenging himself

for his man's plain speaking by giving
him trouble.

But for once he did his employer an
injustice. Mr. Rushton's apathy was
quite genuine. He was in a state of
physical exhaustion which alone would
have caused him to shrink from any exertion ; and he had discovered something
which, for the time, made everything else
appear trifling. What did it matter where
he went, or when, to a man that had just
found out that he was dying ?

That was the fact which had flashed
upon him with all the force of a revelation.
He had talked of sickness before, and of
his end as drawing near, but it had been
merely talk ; he had not seriously believed
that his life was threatened. With the
strange power mortals possess of befooling
themselves, he had shut his eyes to the

symptoms of mortal disease, and had persuaded himself that there was nothing
wrong that could not be set right by
change and skilful treatment.

Now the fell sergeant had touched him
unmistakably, and he knew that the redhot
pincers which had been torturing him
would do him to death. The certainty
of the nearness of death was dreadful
enough in the first freshness of realization ;
but he could have borne that with com-
parative fortitude—few human beings are
not able to summon up courage to face
with dignity the inevitable approach of the
last enemy. It was the manner of his end
that appalled him. He would have to go
through agonies of pain, and he was of a
sensitive nervous organization which made
him dread physical suffering even more
than most men do. His attendants would

have a hard task; and as he foresaw the time when he would be an object of shrinking pity, the vanity which was the very essence of his nature smarted cruelly. No shred of self-complacency would be left him then.

The darkness before him was unrelieved by any ray of comfort. Gay would care for him dutifully; he had no doubt of that, but the certainty was powerless to soothe him. Even if he had been sure that her ministrations would be inspired by the tenderest love, it would have availed him nothing. To care for affection in itself one must have an affectionate nature, which Mr. Rushton had not. The pleasure which he had found hitherto in the society of his family had consisted chiefly in the indulgence of the flattering belief that he was the object of admiration; he would

never have found any sweetness in attach
ment which he could not imagine to be a
tribute to his powers of fascination, and
the prospect of helpless dependence on
his daughter in the state to which he must
come was only horrible to him.

As he dwelt upon the future, the thought
of Pelter troubled him grievously.   A few
hours before he had considered the man
as much his tool and property as if he
had bought him.   Pelter had been in his
confidence in most of his transactions, and
had been useful in a variety of ways ; he
had followed him to England and had
shared his seclusion there.   All at once
the useful machine had become a danger.
Since he had learnt that " the good devoted
fellow " regarded him with dislike and
contempt, a dread of the man had taken
hold of him.   It was not blind devotion

that had bound Pelter to him—what
then was his motive for his faithful
service ? Mr. Rushton had a large sum
of money and some valuable securities,
which he thought it expedient to have
in his own keeping, and he felt sure
that Pelter was only biding his time to
plunder him. That was the reason why
he wished that Gay should not be with
her father. He was afraid that her presence might make it less easy to carry
out his plans. But he would not hesitate at any means of compassing his end.
When pain grew unbearable and Mr.
Rushton must have relief in stupefaction,
Pelter would have no difficulty in murdering him unsuspected. That was the
fear which haunted his mind persistently
during the long hours of the night. He
could not sleep, his weariness was too

great, and his feverishly excited brain con-
jured up again and again a picture of
Pelter murdering him.

The next day, when Susan had finished
her usual work at Kelvers, Pelter told
her he was going away on business, and
would not return till the afternoon of
the morrow, and asked her to spend the
rest of that day and the whole of the next
at the house.   Susan acquiesced rather
reluctantly, for Pelter had inspired her
with a wholesome fear of his master.

Pelter reassuringly informed her that
she need not be afraid.   Mr. Brown was
very quiet just then, and so long as he
was not irritated by any neglect on her
part he would be amiable.

"Don't keep him waiting when he
rings—he gets awfully impatient if that
happens," he impressed upon her.

Then he entered his employer's presence, and informed him of the arrangement he had made.

" You'd better ring for her every now
and then, to make sure she is on the
premises," he remarked. " If she is
kept here all to-day, that will prevent
her from going down to the village
and tattling before Miss Rushton has got
away."

Mr. Rushton did not reply ; he had
scarcely seemed to listen.

" Pelter," he said abruptly, " if you
dislike the idea of going with me, why
should you go ? I will give you a good
sum, if you prefer to stay in England."

" Thank you, no ; that wouldn't quite
suit my book. It was Miss Rushton I
said didn't want to go with you. I don't
wish to leave you, sir."

"After what you said yesterday, I should have thought you *did* wish it. I always meant to leave you comfortable, and you could have the money now."

"You're very kind, but I shall stick by you as long as Miss Rushton is with you."

"Why, what has she to do with it?"

"She'll need somebody at hand to help her."

Mr. Rushton laughed so derisively that for once Pelter's wooden composure was upset.

"Yes, I know I'm barely fit to speak to her, but I can run her errands and carry parcels for her, and prevent you from wearing her out too fast with your unreasonable ways," he said fiercely. "And that's what I mean to do, sir."

He went away, and Susan from the

back door watched him striding over the moor. He was going to Alverthwaite, where he had to pay one or two accounts, which must be settled before their departure ; and he meant also to get some things for Gay's comfort on the journey. She could not provide proper wraps herself, and Mr. Rushton would not think of such a trifling detail. Pelter intended to escort her on her night journey—it should be his first duty in the service he had undertaken towards her — and he would return next day to travel with his master.

Mr. Rushton was left feeling that all his fears were confirmed. Pelter was not to be got rid of by the heaviest bribe, and he shivered at the thought of the danger which he must drag about with him. Life could not be long for him in any case,

and could not show him any good again ;
yet it was dreadful to imagine an assassin
watching for the moment to give him
the last dose, to imagine himself dying
poisoned like a rat in a hole.

It was characteristic that he gave no
credit to the motive Pelter had assigned
for staying, and did not hope that Gay
would exercise any influence over him.
He was never inclined to believe in
generous or disinterested motives, and
he took Pelter's profession of devotion
to Gay as a pretence to cover his real
reason. He had certainly believed that
Pelter would do anything for *him*, but
that was a different thing. Few people
are strong-minded enough to apply their
cynical maxims rigidly to themselves.

It was even more characteristic of Mr.
Rushton that he felt not the faintest hope

or wish that Pelter had spoken the truth, and never reflected that a faithful servant might be very valuable in the future to his daughter. Gay's future was a blank to him, except in so far as it coincided with his; as to what should come after, he had never taxed his imagination, and he was too much absorbed then in his own wretchedness to give a thought to anything of less importance.

It was a gloomy day. The wind moaned round the lonely house, and mist blotted out the surrounding country. Unconscious of the outer world, Mr. Rushton sat blankly contemplating his own mischance. It was not a nightmare—not a fancy of illness— it was sober fact that this hideous fate was confronting him; and bit by bit he realized what it meant—saw himself stripped, first of all that made life pleasant to him, then of all that could make it endurable.

He thought of the future, as he had planned it only two days before. He had meant to do a great deal when he was once more out in the world; he had plenty of projects in his head, but they had shrunk into nothingness now. It was all over. He could scheme no longer; *Finis* was written across his page, and he had not energy enough to try to crowd in a line or two above that grim inscription.

What good would it do him to strive to make a little more money in the time remaining? What flavour would there be in success or luck which came when the last sands were running out? Any such effort would only press more closely home the horror of his condition. Better give up the whole thing at once; he was dead now, to all intents and purposes, and it was mockery to attempt to act as if he had the interests of a living man.

In the afternoon another fit of pain came on, which lasted longer and was more severe than that of the day before— pain which turned existence into a purgatory. "And this is only the beginning," he thought, when it was over; "it will get worse and worse."

Then an idea rose in his mind which was familiar enough to him, but seemed now something new and fresh—"He himself could his quietus make." He had played with the suggestion when he was in some strait, but never before had it come close and spoken seriously. He took out his revolver and looked at it with a strange interest. He would rather die by his own hand than by Pelter's.

Again and again the thought came back to him, and each time it wore a fairer face. He was not quite helpless; he had this means of escape from the ruins into which his life had fallen. Nobody would regret him, he told himself bitterly. Gay would be glad to hear that he was out of the way, and it was all safe for Sophy; she cared infinitely more for her stepmother than for her father.

Presently he looked at his watch, and calculated how long it would be before the woman left in charge would go. Then would be his time to defy fate. Gay and Pelter had been contemptuous when he talked of putting an end to himself; they would find that their scorn was misplaced.

END OF VOL. II.

PRINTED BY WILLIAM CLOWES AND SONS, LIMITED,
LONDON AND BECCLES.